INSTRUCTIONS
FOR A
SECOND-HAND
HEART

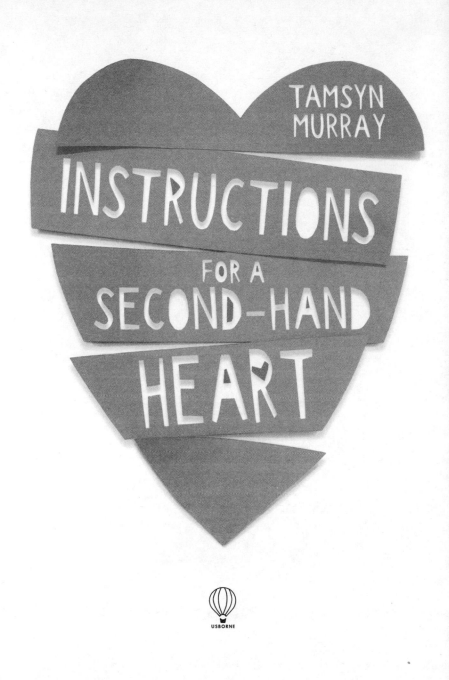

TAMSYN
MURRAY

INSTRUCTIONS
FOR A
SECOND-HAND
HEART

USBORNE

1

JONNY

My name is Jonny Webb and I am a robot.

Last summer, my heart stopped for three and a half minutes.

When they got it going again, the muscle was damaged and didn't work properly. So now I have this machine plugged into me, keeping me alive. It's called a Berlin Heart and you can actually see my blood being pumped along its tubes into these two little round things and then back into my body, which is gross but fascinating. Sometimes, when I can't sleep, I pretend I'm Iron Man and the Berlin Heart is my arc reactor. I know; tragic, right? I'm almost fifteen, the oldest patient in the hospital to have one – all the others are little kids or even babies.

On a good day, I might sketch them as hard-core X-Men characters. On bad days, they remind me that I'm dying.

Being under a death sentence sucks. If you were a smart-arse, you might point out that *everyone* is dying but trust me, I'll be doing it sooner than most. I've spent more than half my life in hospital and every day, I get closer to shooting the breeze with Death.

What I really need is a new heart. But it's not like you can just pick one up down the high street or online. No, you have to wait for someone who matches you to die. Then you have to hope they're on the Organ Donor Register. If they're not, it's up to their family to decide whether to donate any organs that are still up to the job. Not everyone says yes, so there's a massive waiting list. And that's why I think I'll be dead soon, although I don't ever say that around my family. Deep down, we all know it's pretty much a given – I've got this really rare blood type, which reduces the chances of finding a match even more. But we pretend that's not how it is.

My best mate at the hospital is called Emily – aka my only mate these days, because there's only so long you can expect your healthy friends to stick around before you slip gradually out of their minds. Em's got acute myeloid leukaemia and they're not sure she's going to make it either. The hospital psychologists we have to see each week told us to make a list of things to do when we get well

– the opposite of a bucket list – because they reckon it helps to stay positive. Em and I did ours together. It has stupid stuff on it, like *Meet Sam Claflin* (that's hers, not mine – she's got posters of him *everywhere*) and *Meet comic legend Chris Claremont at London Super Comic Con*, 'cos if you're going to dream, you might as well dream big. But there's some not-so-crazy stuff on there too, things most teenagers take for granted, like going to the cinema or moshing at a gig. I'd like to do the whole cinema experience with Em someday – loading up on snacks, getting annoyed at the people who talk, appreciating the action on a big screen. Not like on a date, obviously; I've never fancied Em. She's just someone I can talk to when I feel down, someone who gets what living under a death sentence is like – no one understands you like another hospital kid. It'd be nice to share some good times with Em too.

So here I am, killing time and waiting for exactly the right person to die in exactly the right way. Sometimes, I wish the surgeons could remove my real heart and leave me with this artificial one for ever. Then I wouldn't find myself wishing for a tragedy to happen to someone I've never met. I'd be *genuinely* heartless then, instead of only feeling like I am.

The truth is, I'm not Iron Man. I'm just a boy with no future.

2

NIAMH

"**R**ace you to the rocks!"

Leo stands poised on the shingle beach, his body angled towards a stack of boulders cowering at the base of the limestone cliffs, daring me to run. I scowl and decide to ignore him. Leo might be my twin but we're totally different, inside and out. He's bright and boisterous, like a half-grown Labrador, all big brown eyes and golden hair and enthusiasm – fifteen going on five. And of course, he's popular; everyone loves him, especially the moronic girls at school. People do a double take when they find out we're twins, as though they can't believe we're even related. It's like he nicked all the good stuff while we were in the womb and I got what was left.

He flashes a teasing grin my way. "What's the matter, little sister? Scared I'll beat you again?"

Little sister. He says that a lot, like those three minutes make him Gandalf or something. Mum lifts her sunglasses, pushing her coppery hair back from her face, and glances back and forth between us. She's smiling, but there's anxiety behind her eyes, as though she senses the rage bubbling under my skin. Sometimes, I wonder if she reads my mind. I hope for her sake she doesn't. It's a dark place these days.

Her forehead crinkles into a frown and I feel bad. This holiday is her attempt at fixing things – a reminder of the sun-drenched beach adventures of our childhood, when the two of us spent the days playing pirates and exploring rock pools, and the nights squashed side by side in our tiny caravan bunks – inseparable. Then we got older and the cracks began to appear. Leo became the family golden boy – ace footballer, A* student and everybody's mate. No matter how hard I tried, I was never as good. Once I'd fallen into his shadow I couldn't find my way out and, eventually, I stopped trying.

My gaze settles on the sea, sparkling in the mid-afternoon heat haze, and the man walking his dog along the frothing surf. I should make the effort and pretend I'm not actually a seething mass of resentment.

My stomach churns as I consider the options. Play nicely

or pick a fight? Mum's tension is obvious now and I feel sick, as though everyone's happiness hinges on what I do next. Fight or flight, they call it in science, the body's reaction to stress and Leo definitely stresses me out. I don't really hate him but like a certain social networking site says, it's complicated. I can't say I like him, either.

"Don't be a knob all your life, Leo," I say, turning away.

"Niamh!" Mum exclaims, sounding disappointed. Out of the corner of my eye, I see Leo's smile falter. And in that split second, when his shoulders droop in defeat, *that's* when I run, speeding past him in a spray of pebbles. He lets out a yell of surprise and then I hear him crunching after me.

He's close. I can hear his breath ragged in my ear, a gurgle of laughter underneath it. But for all his boasting, we're a pretty even match; he's big but I'm speedy, and the precious few seconds' head start I have is enough to keep me in the lead. The breeze sends my hair streaming out behind me and tickles my face, at the same time as my muscles stretch and sing. I realize with a jolt that I'm actually enjoying myself. I don't do sport. In fact, I don't really do *anything* so I'm amazed my body knows how to react. But it feels good. Heaving in a deep breath, I urge my legs to move faster and focus on my goal. I have to win. I have to.

The rocks are close now – I can see they're wet and half-covered in seaweed. Something brushes the back of my faded Smiths T-shirt – Leo's fingers. And that's about right too – everyone thinks he's Mr Perfect but he's not above a bit of cheating to get what he wants. Not this time, though. Another burst of determination shoots through me and I power forwards. With a grunt of effort, I reach out and slap a waist-high boulder with my hand.

"Winner!"

He crashes into the back of me, sending me sprawling over the rock and knocking what little breath I have left from my lungs. Briny seawater slops over my feet and the hard jagged rock jabs under my ribcage. I let out a surprised *oof* of pain.

His weight lifts, allowing me to push myself up and glare at him.

"Soz," he pants, stepping back with an unrepentant grin. "Couldn't stop."

"Yeah, you could," I say, shaking the water off my Converse. "Loser."

He tips his head, acknowledging the truth. "Okay, you won. But I bet you can't beat me to the top!"

God, he really is a five-year-old. He means the cluster of rocks, which is bigger than it seemed from the other side of the beach, jutting over our heads in a mini-mountain beneath the clifftop. They're jumbled together every which way, the razor-sharp edges dressed with slick seaweed and algae. I hesitate.

"Of course, if you're too scared…"

He leaves the words hanging in the heat, knowing as well as I do that he doesn't need to finish the sentence. Inextricably tangled up in my resentment and irritation is a tiny spark of competitiveness I can't quite extinguish, the need to prove something. Sometimes it's a battle in my head, like beating him to the last Pop-Tart. Today, it's this and I can see from his face that he thinks he's already won.

"Let's make it interesting," I say, my mind searching for a way to get the upper hand. "If I win, I get your guitar."

I don't actually want it, I just want to threaten something he loves. He fancies himself as a musician, reckons he'll make it one day, and no one is allowed to touch his precious Fender. I honestly think he loves it more than he loves his girlfriend. The threat has the desired effect, anyway – his eyes narrow. "Get lost, Niamh. Like you'd know what to do with it."

A gust of wind whips my hair across my face and I taste sand as I lick my lips. "Now who's scared?"

We stare at each other and something flashes between us; pride, understanding? It's gone before I can work out what it is. But I know Leo won't back down.

"All right. And if I win, you have to get down on your knees and admit that I am awesome."

The realization that I literally have nothing he wants rubs salt in an already open wound. Twin spots of humiliation burn my cheeks. "It's never going to happen but okay."

He fires a mocking smile my way. "Ready to lose?"

My legs tense once more and, this time, there's an added tingle. I nod.

"On your marks, get set, go!"

He's off, white Vans scrambling over the slippery surface as he scales the boulders immediately in front of us. My gaze travels sideways and spots an easier, flatter route. I jog a few metres to the right and start to climb.

At first, I think I've made a mistake. Leo is much higher than me and I feel like I'm going sideways instead of up. Then he stops, surveying the rocks above him. Lip curling, I concentrate on my own path. Behind us, there's a faint shout. I glance back to see Mum and Dad heading our way. Mum has her arm in the air, waving, and I can imagine her worried expression. All the more reason to hurry, I decide; she's bound to make us come down when she gets nearer. Leo looks my way, grinning, and I guess he's thinking the same thing. We both climb faster.

We're almost level when I notice him pause again. My strategy is paying off; the top boulder is in sight and the rocks ahead of me look like an easy climb. Leo stands still, his feet precariously balanced either side of an evil-looking ridge, and I can see why he's stopped. There's a gaping hole between where he stands and the next rock. If he wants to beat me, he'll have to jump.

His gaze flickers downwards, as though he's considering

backtracking. A surge of triumph rushes through me; if he does that, there's no way he can win.

"Sucks to be you, Leo," I call across to him, scaling the stone with the kind of spidery skill that would put Peter Parker to shame. "How much do you think your guitar will fetch on eBay?"

He scowls and scans the rocks with more urgency. Laughing, I manoeuvre past the last obstacle in my way and clamber onto the top of the rocks. Below, I hear a grunt. I look down, just as Leo clears the gap and grips onto the rock above. But there's something wrong. I see panic on his face. His fingers scrabble in the half-dried seaweed and his feet scratch against the stone, struggling to hold his weight. He hangs there, almost floating. Without a thought, I throw myself down flat and thrust out a hand to grab him. My fingers grip his and in a whoosh of relief, I've got him. But a second later he slips through my grasp and I'm holding thin air. He starts to drop. My terrified gaze locks onto his as he falls, almost in slow motion. Then there's the sickening crunch of bone on rock and his eyelids snap shut.

He lies unmoving. I watch red blossom against the grey-black boulder where his head rests. And somewhere, somebody starts to scream.

3

JONNY

"Can I get you anything, love?"

Mum is hovering at my side, the way she does most days, her face tired and careworn. She looks older than her fifty-five years, something she can thank me for – I've worried her for most of my life. I know they'd almost given up on a baby by the time I came along so it seems cruel that the one they got was faulty. Dad looks old, too, although they both try to keep in shape. Dad used to run marathons. He doesn't any more.

I shake my head. "No thanks."

She reaches out to take a grape from the bag on my table. "These are good. Want one?"

This time, I turn away. "No."

Sometimes my mother drives me insane. Dad is here less so he doesn't get on my nerves as much. To be fair, most of the time, they're pretty good at picking up when I want to be alone and they wander off to the canteen, but Mum obviously has her irritation detector switched off today. One of the worst things about spending 24/7 in hospital is that it's a bit like being in *Big Brother*, but without the Z-list status and shopping tasks – there's always someone who wants to "take a quick look" at you, poking and prodding like you're a laboratory experiment. And everyone on your ward knows everything about you, even the little kids; there's no such thing as privacy. We have this traffic light system over our beds to let people know if we feel like being sociable – a green card means "party on", amber means "tread carefully" and red means "do not disturb", which my mother usually ignores. Em's is red a lot because the chemo makes her vom, but she sometimes makes an exception for me. That's when I dig out my funniest jokes, because it turns out laughter really is the best medicine. I know hearing Em laugh always makes *me* feel better.

"I see Manesh has gone home," Mum says, clearly determined to get me talking. "Such a lovely family. I'm glad things worked out for them."

Manesh is the nine-year-old boy who, until this morning, occupied the bed opposite mine. Things get pretty intense on the ward – the families lean on one another for support and celebrate the successes just as hard as they mourn the losses. It was touch and go with Manesh for a while so I can't begrudge him his happy ending; it's not as though he's the first kid on the ward to get a transplant before me, the common blood groups are easier to match up with donors, although the hearts need to be the right size. Even so, I can't manage much more than a grunt in reply.

"Nick says you're at the top of the transplant list," Mum persists. "It'll be your turn next."

Nick is my transplant coordinator and he's been telling me I'll get a heart soon for so long that I don't believe him any more. My immune system is sensitized, which means my body would attack some tissue types, so the doctors can't do anything until the right heart comes up and every day I spend on my Berlin Heart increases my chances of an infection or having a stroke. Blood is pretty clever stuff, it knows when it's outside of the body and it doesn't like it. So the blood in the Berlin Heart tries to clot. If that happens, the chamber has to be changed for a new one. One day, the stroke could be severe and I'll run out of chances.

"It's not really up to Nick," I reply, turning to look at my mother. "He's not God."

She smiles, indulging my grumpiness like she always does. "It's your turn next. I know it is."

I want to scream then, because she knows no such thing. Mum has a degree in staying cheerful and mostly, it's easier to go along with her. But sometimes – just sometimes – I wish she'd drop the "Everything Is Awesome" act and face the truth: she doesn't have to worry about what to get me for Christmas. But then I look into her eyes and see how much she needs to believe and all my irritation drains away.

"Maybe just one grape," I say, reaching for the bag.

Em stops by after tea.

"What's going on with you today?" she asks, sitting down next to my bed and arranging her drip stand. "Too cool for school?"

She grins as she says it, showing me she's not being snarky, and I see her lips are red and sore with ulcers. You'd think being sick means we get out of lessons and stuff but no such luck. The hospital has its own school although we don't have to go every day if we don't want to. Sometimes, if you don't feel well, a teacher comes to you for a bit instead. It's not as horrific as it sounds; most of the people who work here are pretty cool. My favourite is a nurse called Femi who brings me the coolest manga comics ever. I've shown him some of my own drawings and he reckons I'm good enough to maybe get a job as an illustrator someday. I haven't bothered to point out that "someday" will probably never happen.

"You know how it is." I look at Em. "I didn't fancy it."

I don't mention that I've felt weird all day, sluggish and weary and unsociable. I haven't even felt like drawing – my sketchbook lies unopened on the bed. Em and I have a pact – total honesty – but she has it worse than me most of the time and I don't want to moan.

She knows me too well, though. "What? Is it another infection?"

The Berlin Heart means I have open wounds in my chest where the tubes come in and out of my body, which means infection is never far away. But I don't think that's it, I don't feel feverish or shivery, which are the usual dead giveaways. I just feel...old. "It's probably nothing," I say, trying my hardest to sound casual. "What did I miss today?"

She refuses to be sidetracked. "I'm calling Femi."

"No," I say, sitting up so fast it makes my head spin. "Don't."

"Then tell me what's going on."

I lie back on my pillow. "Do you ever wonder whether it's worth it? All this treatment?"

She stares at me like I've grown another head. "Of course it is."

Ordinarily, I'd agree. But Manesh going home has bothered me more than I want to admit; it's like his good fortune has reminded me how bad my own chances are. So I've been thinking about dying. I've been thinking about it a lot. "It feels like I'm running out of luck, Em."

"Bull," she says briskly. "You're going to outlive me."

The confidence in her voice makes me smile in spite of myself. She's talking crap, of course; after all the chemo she's been through, every cell in her body has been nuked – she must be at least half-superhero by now.

"Maybe."

Em gets up, touches a cool hand to my forehead. "This isn't like you. Are you sure you're not ill?"

It takes a minute for the ridiculousness of what she's just said to sink in, then we both explode into laughter. "God, I'm such an idiot," she gasps eventually. "Sorry."

We cackle like hyenas until Femi pokes his dark head around the curtain. His eyes dance when he sees us laughing. "What's so funny?"

Em waves him away. "You had to be there."

"It was obviously a good joke," he says. "And you know the rules about good jokes."

Femi has the most amazing full-bellied laugh and loves nothing better than to share it, so his rule is that good jokes have to go on the noticeboard. But this wasn't the kind of joke anyone else would laugh at – like Em says, you had to be there. "Sorry, Femi," I say, "it's a private joke. No one else would get it."

He nods. "You two are great friends. It makes my heart glad to see you laughing." His gaze comes to rest on my sketchbook. "Have you been drawing, my friend?"

"Not today," I tell him and reach for the manga book on my bedside table. "I finished the comic you brought me, though."

Em squints at the title. "*Fairy Tail*? Really?"

Femi and I exchange a look. Em doesn't get our shared obsession with manga. In fact, she doesn't really get my comic obsession full stop. Femi does, though. We've secretly agreed that if Em doesn't want to go to London Super Comic Con with me when we're better, then Femi will. If I'm completely honest, I'm kind of hoping Em ducks out of it – she's great but Femi knows every X-Men plot inside out and backwards.

"Ah," he says, stepping forward to take the comic. "You will need *Return of the Dragons!* next. Natsu faces his greatest challenge yet. I will bring it tomorrow."

"Thanks," I say.

"No problem," he replies, his face splitting into a grin. "Make sure you get some rest."

He vanishes behind the curtains. Em yawns and gets to her feet. "I should be going too," she says, pushing her stand towards the gap. "See you tomorrow, yeah? Try not to die in the night."

I smile, because it's another one of our private jokes. "You too."

1

NIAMH

I don't remember a lot of what happens immediately after the accident. I know I get down from the rocks somehow, and the man walking his dog races over to help my white-faced, panic-stricken mother but I couldn't tell you anything he does. And I know my father calls the emergency services, with shaking fingers that take three attempts to dial the numbers, but only because he tells me so afterwards. I remember seeing the air ambulance land on the stony beach, and watching the paramedics take care of Leo, but the seconds after I hear his head smack into the unyielding rock are dark in my mind.

They work on him for half an hour, thirty long minutes of hushed medical jargon while we look on in helpless silence. Dad holds my hand, squeezing hard but I don't complain. Leo doesn't open his eyes once. Part of me expects one eyelid to flicker back, for him to grin when he sees our stressed faces. But another part of me, the bit that wonders how much blood someone can lose before they're in serious trouble, worries that we won't see him laugh again for a long time. And I curse myself for agreeing to his stupid dare; if I'd refused, we'd be on our way back to the cottage by now. I wish I'd taken another route up the rocks, that he hadn't felt the pressure to win and taken a crazy risk. I even wish it was me lying pale and still, except I'd never have had the bottle to try the jump in the first place.

Mum goes with Leo in the helicopter. I think Dad wants to go as well but there isn't room for all of us and someone has to move the car from the beachside pay-and-display car park. So he shakes the hand of the man with the dog and promises to let him know how Leo gets on. We drive to the hospital in silence. I see and don't see the countryside flash by, the speedometer creeping up and up as Dad takes the corners faster than he should. A film of unreality covers everything, like I'm observing events through dusty glass. My scratched hands, folded tightly around Leo's battered phone, don't look like my own. They don't feel like part of me. Nothing does.

At the hospital, we're ushered in to meet Mum. She's in a waiting room, her hair wild and her cheeks colourless, with a nurse at her side. They're talking as we walk in.

"No news yet," Mum says, as Dad wraps her in a hug. "They're assessing him now."

The nurse introduces herself as Kerry and explains she's there to answer our questions. I can only think of one and Mum's already answered it. My parents sit beside each other on a low sofa, holding hands, and not for the first time it strikes me how unlike them Leo and I are. He used to joke that we'd been swapped at birth, and that the real Brody kids looked at their parents with the same confusion as us. Our Mum is petite, with coppery red hair that has tinges of silver if you know where to look and Dad is dark-haired and blue-eyed, a throwback to his Irish roots. They seem smaller as they sit, facing Kerry, diminished by worry. I look away, desperate for something to distract me and my eyes alight on the fish tank in the wall. It's lit soft blue from behind and the movement of the fish is oddly soothing. I can't take my eyes off them, and when I touch the glass, it's warm. Tropical fish, I decide, my eyes following the movements of a black-and-white striped one, zebra-like with fins and a fantail. Letting them hypnotize me is infinitely better than staring at the clinical white walls or butting into the small talk between my parents and Kerry. Better too than seeing the constant replay of Leo dropping away from me.

"How was he in the helicopter?" Dad asks.

Mum's gaze flickers my way, as if she doesn't want me to hear her answer. A flash of annoyance sears through me – she's trying to protect me but it's too late for that. I was right there when Leo fell; I heard the crunch as he landed. And they don't call out the air ambulance for cuts and grazes. I know it's serious.

She lets out a long, unsteady breath and her voice is hardly more than a whisper when she answers. "His heart stopped. They managed to get it going again. He needed a blood transfusion."

The words jolt me as though I've been punched. Why did his heart stop? He hit his head, not his chest. A buzzing starts in my ears and I place both hands on the glass of the tank to steady myself. How bad is he?

I force myself to breathe. Slowly the rushing sound subsides and I try to take in this new information. His heart stopped. His heart *stopped*.

Dad swallows. "That's…good. Good that they got it going again."

Kerry nods. And on one hand I know what Dad means: of course it's good that they got Leo's heart going again. But they shouldn't have needed to. Unless—

"What if there's a blood clot on his brain?" I burst out. "I saw this TV show once where someone hit their head and a blood clot nearly killed them! Is that why his heart stopped?"

"Niamh," Dad groans.

I stare at Kerry, feeling my breath come and go in short, shallow gasps. "Is that what happened?"

Mum covers her face with her hands.

"It's too early to say." Kerry's tone is calm and soothing. "Try not to think the worst at this stage."

The fact that she doesn't deny it causes a stab of panic to scythe through my guts. I want her to tell me not to believe everything I see on TV, that it's exaggerated for the cameras. Instead, it's like she's confirmed my suspicions. I watch a cluster of tiny neon-bright fish race each other across the tank and wish I knew more about head injuries.

We sit, doing nothing, the strained silence punctuated by the occasional question from Mum and Dad. The clock on the wall has pointed to one-fifteen since we arrived; I guess the hospital has bigger priorities than replacing the battery. It feels wrong to check my phone, which means I have no idea how long we've been waiting. Long enough for Leo to wake up? Long enough for them to mend his broken brain? Long enough for his heart to stop beating again?

Kerry goes off to get us some tea. I can't stand the inactivity any longer and take the opportunity to pull out my phone. My hands need something to do but my fingers are clumsy as they stab at the screen and I find it hard to focus; the words swim around like I'm looking at them through the water in the fish tank. Eventually, I stuff the phone back into my pocket and sit picking at a torn fingernail. There's dried blood underneath and I honestly can't tell if it's Leo's or mine.

The door opens. A woman dressed in red scrubs walks in, a stethoscope around her neck. Kerry is behind her with a tray of steaming tea. My parents stand up.

"Mr and Mrs Brody?" the woman asks and they both nod. "Hello, my name is Philippa Ross. I'm one of the A & E consultants."

"How is he?" Dad asks.

I scrutinize her expression for clues. But she's poker-faced, blank and unreadable. I suppose she deals with people like us every day. She waves at us to sit and I join my parents on the sofa. Kerry hands out cardboard cups of tea. I wrap my hands around mine, absorbing the warmth. The room isn't cold but I can't stop shivering. I hope Kerry added plenty of sugar.

"The good news is that his condition is stable," Ms Ross begins. "But his head wound is worrying us. We've stemmed the bleeding and he's on his way for some tests now. Once those are done, we'll know more but –" she pauses and meets my parents' gaze – "I should warn you that his brain function may be impaired."

The cup jerks in Mum's hand. "What do you mean?"

"He's not responding as well as I'd like. The early indications are that the accident may have caused some damage."

The buzzing in my ears intensifies. What kind of damage? Mum closes her eyes and leans into Dad. "How bad is it?"

"It really is too soon to say," Ms Ross says, her voice heavy with sympathy. She gets to her feet. "Leo has been transferred to the intensive care unit now and is undergoing more tests. One of the specialist consultants will come and see you as soon as they can."

Mum and Dad stand up too, and follow her to the door. I stay seated, mostly because I'm not sure my legs will take my weight.

"I really am sorry not to have better news," Ms Ross says, and she looks it. "Kerry will stay with you, in case you need anything."

I pull my knees up and hug them. Kerry touches my arm. "I know you're worried but Leo is in safe hands."

I almost lose it then; I have to look away and breathe... breathe...don't think, just breathe.

The door closes with a sigh. We wait and each passing minute hacks away at my sanity. The fish have lost their calming effect – I don't even see them any more. I think I might snap if I don't do something so I pull my phone out again and concentrate hard on moving my fingers over the screen. Facebook is a haven of normality, which helps – friends and half-friends boasting or moaning about their lives. If I try hard enough, I can almost convince myself everything is fine, until I see Leo's update about chasing the waves at the beach and then all I can see is him dropping away from me, his eyes fixed on mine. My fingers twitch, as though this time they'll stop him from falling, and I flick them over the screen again. Eighty-seven friends have liked his status. I wonder how they'll react when they find out about the accident. Shock first, then I suppose it depends on how bad it is. Ms Ross's words crawl through my head: *He's not responding as well as I'd like...*

Hours go by before the door opens again. This time it's a man who walks in. He's wearing a white shirt and grey trousers and he doesn't smile. My heart constricts. I have a bad feeling, a yawning black abyss where my stomach should be.

"Hello, my name is James Archer. I'm a consultant neurosurgeon at the hospital. I've been helping to care for Leo since he arrived."

Mum's hands twist in her lap as she clears her throat. "Thank you for looking after him. Is – is there any news?"

There must be or he wouldn't be here. But all of a sudden, I don't want to hear whatever this unsmiling man has to say, don't want the bubble of possibility to be burst. It's like that Schrödinger's Cat theory we studied in physics, where there's a cat locked in a box with some poison and no one knows if the poison has killed it until someone opens the box, so it's simultaneously alive and dead. In that moment, I understand the theory completely – both possibilities are true as long as we don't lift the lid. But we can't stay in limbo for long. James Archer is going to impose one reality or the other, whether we want it or not.

He meets my parents' anxious stares squarely. "It's not good." His voice softens and slows. "Our initial tests indicate that the fall caused some catastrophic damage to Leo's brainstem. I'm sorry to say it looks extensive."

Mum sucks in a long, shuddering breath. Beside her, Dad slumps back against the sofa. "What does that mean?" he asks.

"It means we need to do more tests," Mr Archer says. "Once we know how much damage there is, we can talk about what's best for Leo."

What's best for Leo is for the doctors to fix him, but I'm suddenly terrified that they can't. My eyes fill with tears that drop, unheeded, onto my phone and I barely notice when Kerry lifts it from my unresisting fingers.

"The tests will take some time," he goes on. "It's possible we may not have the results for several hours yet."

"Can we see him though?" Mum asks, her voice thick.

"Of course," the consultant says, without hesitation. "I should warn you that you'll see a lot of tubes and wires from the machines and drips."

A fresh wave of unreality washes over me. Drips and wires and machines...this can't be happening. I'm not even sure I want to see Leo; I don't want to open the box and face the evidence. But at the same time I need to see him and I am glad Mum asked.

Mr Archer stands. "I'll take you to him now, if you're ready?"

I'm not ready. I'll never be ready. But I follow them out of the room anyway.

5

JONNY

I know something is wrong the moment I wake up. I can't move my arm, can't reach the button to call the nurses. I try to shout for help but the words don't come out right – they're thick and slow. Eventually, I manage to knock my water jug to the floor, where it clatters loudly. A frowning nurse comes to investigate and everything happens very quickly from then. There are tests and more tests and it turns out a clot has escaped from my Berlin Heart. It's gone into my bloodstream, causing a mini stroke – dangerous but not as damaging as a full stroke. What it does mean is a new heart chamber, more medicines injected into my many tubes and more hushed conversations just out of earshot. Seriously, if I had the strength I'd throw something; a pee bottle, a monitor, a tantrum – *anything* to make them see that there's more to me than just a crap heart.

"They're worried about their investment," Em says when she's allowed to see me, much later. "That machine might as well be made out of bling it costs so much money."

She means the Berlin Heart – as treatments go, it's pretty costly and I've had mine a year, which Em reckons makes me the most expensive patient the hospital has ever had. Another time that might make me feel better, if her words weren't tinged with pity. See, when a girl with no hair and a mouthful of ulcers feels sorry for you, you know you're in trouble.

The mini stroke means my parents spend the whole day here, watching me closely for after-effects. I don't know how they do it; I can't think of anything more boring than cleaning the wounds where the tubes go in and out and watching me sleep but they don't complain. God knows how Dad gets so much time off work – maybe he's been sacked and doesn't want me to know. He does his best to stay cheerful but I can see the strain on his face, the not-quite-hidden worry in Mum's eyes. Actually, I can't remember the last time I looked at them and didn't see fear.

Femi stops by to see how I am and brings me a couple of comics. We don't talk about the mini stroke much.

It's my third since I got my Berlin Heart so I'm pretty used to them by now but every time it happens, I play the odds. Next time, the clot could be bigger and the effects might be permanent.

That's the thing about living on borrowed time. Eventually it runs out.

6

NIAMH

Leo's room is quiet, or as quiet as it can be with the ventilator whooshing noisily and a hundred monitors beeping every other second. A nurse is making notes on a clipboard as Mr Archer leads us in. They have a brief, hushed conversation, and then, with a sad-eyed smile at us, she leaves.

Leo is utterly still among the white cotton sheets. His chest rises evenly, in time with the ventilator but that's the only movement. It sounds stupid but I think his stillness bothers me most; I'm used to Leo being active and full of life, like Tigger on a sugar rush. He even used to sleepwalk. I could try to kid myself that he's asleep now, I suppose, except that the tube taped to his mouth, and the beeps, and the jagged spike of the heart monitor are a constant reminder that he's not.

Mum looks at Mr Archer and I see her eyes glittering with unshed tears under the dim lights. "Can I touch him?"

"Of course."

She steps up to the bed and gazes down. I don't know how she can be so strong. She reaches out to smoothe his hair, a gesture I know he'd hate, and I see that one side of his head is shaved. There's a small, neatly stitched wound there. I can't believe that something the size of a twenty-pence piece could have such devastating consequences. But then I can't believe any of what's happened.

Dad is beside her. Mum rests against him and they stand together, silent.

"Is there anything you'd like to ask?" Mr Archer says.

Mum looks back, her lips a thin line, making me wonder if she can't trust herself to speak. But she shakes her head. Dad shows no sign he even heard. I have so many questions that I feel sick from holding them all in. But at the same time I'm afraid of hearing the answers.

Mr Archer clears his throat respectfully. "I'll give you some time alone."

The door clicks softly behind him. After a few moments, Mum glances over at me and I see her face is puffy.

"This must be so hard for you," she says, her hand seeking mine.

It is; hard and unfair and devastating, in a thousand ways that keep on rolling in like suffocating waves. But the last thing she needs is to worry about me. I do my best to dredge up a smile, with muscles that feel numb. "I'm okay. You know."

She nods and I want her to pull me close and make everything better, like she did when we were little. But already I can see her thoughts drifting back to Leo, so I let my hand drop away, freeing her to go to him. Dad follows. They stand beside the bed, Mum's fingers fussing with Leo's hair, the bedding, the improbably patterned hospital gown he wears, as though these little gestures of love can somehow heal him.

"He looks so peaceful," Mum says. Her voice catches on the last word and she's crying again. Maybe she's tormenting herself about the accident; should she have stopped us? She might as well have tried to stop the sun from shining. Whereas I could have prevented all of this; if we hadn't raced, we wouldn't be here.

"He'll be okay," Dad says. "He's strong. A fighter. We'll get through this."

But looking at Leo now, so pale and still, I find it hard to believe he'll ever be the same. A sense of dread creeps over me as I remember Mr Archer's words: *Once we know how much damage there is, we can talk about what's best for Leo...*

I have no idea how long it is before Mr Archer comes

back but my legs are aching from standing up. There's a chair by the bed I could sit in, I guess, if I wasn't so restless. He's not alone this time; Kerry is with him and an older woman who I assume is another doctor. Suddenly the room feels small and crowded.

"We'd like to start Leo's tests now," Mr Archer says, after he's introduced the doctor. "As I explained, they'll take some time. You're welcome to wait in the family room, or perhaps get a hot drink or a snack." He checks the time. "The cafe is open late – I can ask someone to show you the way if you'd like?"

I can't bear the thought of eating but suddenly I realize how thirsty I am. The tea Kerry brought us was hours ago. "I need a drink."

Kerry pokes her head out of the door, then leaves. Moments later, she's back with another nurse. "Joe will take you to the cafe."

Mum nods but she stays by Leo's side, his hand in hers. "You'll tell us as soon as there's news?"

"Yes," Mr Archer says. "I'll find you."

Dad puts his arm around Mum to guide her out. She doesn't want to go – her fingers hold on to Leo until the very last second – but eventually she lets herself be shepherded to the door.

"Back soon, Leo," she calls, and her voice only cracks on the final letter.

The clock in the cafe says nine o'clock. There aren't any seats, just a counter covered in cellophane-wrapped snacks and a till, with a shiny chrome coffee machine behind it and an employee who looks like he wants to be anywhere else. Mum and Dad have tea. I get a Coke, which tastes too sweet, and then Joe leads us back to the family room.

The clock in here still says one-fifteen. My phone battery died ages ago, in spite of the uncharacteristic lack of use, so I have no idea whether time is crawling by as slowly as it seems to be. Dad closes his eyes and pretty soon he's dozing, although it's a watchful sleep. Mum sits staring into space, dull-eyed and silent. I have nothing to say, no words of comfort to offer her. It feels like all I can do to keep breathing.

My eyes are gritty with exhaustion when Mr Archer comes to see us again. Kerry is with him, and another woman. She's not in a nurse's uniform like Kerry – another doctor, maybe? My head starts to swim as the three of them sit down.

"Mr and Mrs Brody," Mr Archer says. "Niamh. I'd like to introduce you to Narinder. She's a specialist nurse who works with us here."

Narinder presses her lips together in a small smile but doesn't speak. *Why isn't she in uniform?* I wonder. *What kind of nurse is she?* But I don't have time to worry about her for long because Mr Archer is speaking again.

"As you know, we've been undertaking some tests on Leo's brain to establish how much damage the fall caused." He pauses and gazes at each of us in turn. "I am so very sorry but the results of these tests are beyond doubt. We aren't seeing any brain function at all."

"What?" Dad says, his face growing even more ashen. "But how can that be? He's asleep, still breathing."

I know what it means. No brain function means game over.

Mr Archer draws in a deep breath. "I am very sorry. Leo's brain is dead, and without it he can't survive. It might look like he's alive but that's just the machines. Leo is gone."

"Did…did he ever wake up?" Mum asks, her voice breaking a little. She's not crying, not yet, but her face is sickly white and the shadows under her eyes are spreading like grey bruises.

The consultant shakes his head. "He never regained consciousness. From what we can tell, brain death was instantaneous, the moment he hit the rocks. He wouldn't have known what was happening."

That's easy for him to say. He didn't see the flash of panic in Leo's eyes as he fell, imagine the plea for help he didn't have time to scream. But I need to believe that he had no idea what was coming and so I push the memory away.

Now Mum's tears spill over. "It didn't h-h-hurt, then?"

Dad is crying too, and even Kerry's eyes are glistening.

"He wouldn't have felt any pain," Mr Archer soothes, his eyes never leaving us. "I really am so very sorry."

Mum buries her face in Dad's shoulder and sobs. He looks at me through wet eyelashes and stretches out an arm, drawing me into his other side. I'm not into physical contact and it's been years since I hugged either of my parents but now, for this one moment, it feels like the right place to be.

Kerry holds out a box of tissues she's acquired from somewhere. Dad takes one for Mum, one for himself. I wipe my face but it's slick with tears again almost immediately. James Archer waits in silence and I feel a surge of anger at his calmness. "The last doctor said Leo was stable. Maybe he just needs time."

"We could allow more time," he replies. "But he was unresponsive to every test we undertook. I'm afraid there's no doubt."

His implacable expression infuriates me more, as does my parents' meek acceptance, their apparent refusal to fight for Leo. "So operate," I snap. "Do something instead of giving up. Do your job."

I sound shrill and unreasonable even to my own ears but Mr Archer stays patient. "Believe me, if there was even the slightest hope that Leo might recover, I would operate. But we've done all the tests and my colleagues and I agree

– the damage is irreversible. Leo's brain function won't ever return."

I turn to Dad and squeeze my eyes shut. Hot, impotent tears leak out of the sides. I can't believe this is happening – I was squabbling with Leo over breakfast only a few hours ago and now we're supposed to accept that he's dead, even though he's not.

"At least he didn't suffer," Dad says eventually, the words forced and choked. "At least it was quick."

Mum's head bobs up and down in a way that makes me suspect she's struggling to get much comfort from that knowledge. We're not religious, there's no talk of him being in a better place now, as though life is some sort of test and you get the real deal if you pass. I imagine plenty of well-meaning people will reassure us that Leo is with the angels, over the weeks to come. And who knows, his loss might be easier to bear if we believe them.

"There is one more thing," Mr Archer says in a slow, measured voice, and we all look at him. "Because of the nature of Leo's accident, most of his body is uninjured and we have to think about what happens now. I know this is difficult for you to think about but I wondered whether you'd ever discussed organ donation with Leo."

I gasp, unable to stop myself. It feels like a sick joke – Leo is still breathing, his heart is still beating, and they want to cut him open to save someone else? My parents look equally shocked. Dad opens his mouth and I'm sure he's going to tell this doctor where to shove his organ donation but then Mum speaks. "Yes," she says, her voice sounding as though it's coming from a long way away, "as a matter of fact we did."

A memory stirs, of us all sitting around late one night watching one of those police reality shows where they raid people's houses for a bit of weed or pull people over for doing forty in a thirty zone. An accident appeared on screen, the kind where it's obvious someone isn't going to make it, prompting a conversation about whether we wanted our parts to be donated when we died. Selfishly, I'd panicked at the idea and said no. Leo, of course, had done the opposite.

"Think about the people you could help," he'd said, his eyes briefly serious. "The lives you might save. I'd want to make a difference, wouldn't you?"

I'd felt even smaller than usual then, until he'd smirked. "Besides, have you seen me? Seems a shame to waste such a quality product."

Mr Archer glances at Narinder and suddenly I know why she's here. A specialist nurse, he called her – she's obviously a specialist in persuading people to give up their loved ones' organs.

"Narinder has a lot of expertise in this area," the consultant says. "She can help you to decide what's best for Leo."

The specialist nurse dips her head. "I want you to know how sorry I am. This is a terrible time for you, especially when Leo still seems very much alive." She pauses and gazes at us with compassionate eyes. "But you should also know that he can't feel pain. He isn't aware of anything. Leo is gone."

Mum is looking at Dad and it's as though they're having this unspoken conversation. I can't believe they're even considering it – what if the doctors are wrong and there's a chance Leo might wake up? It's too soon to be thinking of something so final. What if? *What if?* And then I look at Mr Archer. His face is grave and sad but, above all, certain. Acceptance starts to seep into my heart.

"Leo could help to save and change so many lives," Narinder continues. "What you need to decide now is whether that's something he would have wanted."

Mum sucks in a breath; a guttural, sticky snort full of desolation. Dad turns to her, his face wet with tears. And Mum holds out a hand to me, her one remaining child, making me part of what happens next, even though I don't want to be.

We sit, our hands clasped together. My mind skitters back to that evening, where we talked about organ donation. "Wouldn't you want someone to do that for you, if you were ill?" Leo asked. "To give you a shot at living?"

I'd made some flippant reply, because it all seemed

distant and improbable and I'd thought he was full of crap anyway. But now here we are and suddenly I don't think he was full of crap at all – he was serious. So what I feel doesn't matter.

Taking a deep breath, I squeeze my parents' hands and a flash of understanding passes between us. Just like that, the decision is made.

"Can we stay with him tonight?" Mum asks. "At least for a little while?"

"Of course," Mr Archer says.

Mum stares at the floor. Her gaze rests there for so long that I wonder if she's having second thoughts. She looks at Dad one final time and he dips his head in agreement. Mum's voice is steady when she speaks. "Then take what you need."

The consultant presses his lips together and Narinder nods. "I'll be here to help and support you every step of the way."

It's done.

And somehow, in among the fury and the shock and the howling unfairness, it feels right.

7

NIAMH

There is paperwork to be done, of course, and question after question about Leo's life. They say we'll get a letter telling us which organs are taken. It feels macabre to me, but Mum and Dad seem comforted and I suppose to them, knowing his death will change lives is the tiny chink of light in the darkness. Which is typical Leo really – even now, he's still the golden boy.

Finally, all the questions are answered and the consent forms signed. And now that it comes down to it, I wish there was something else to keep us busy, something to put off what's coming next.

Leo looks just the same as before. It's so hard to believe he won't open his eyes and smile ever again. There's a tangerine blanket over his legs, tucked in neatly at the corners. The thought of someone taking such care to keep him warm when they must have known there was no real need nearly sets me off again and I clamp my cheek between my teeth. One of my unwritten rules is never to give Leo the satisfaction of seeing me cry and although everything has changed, old habits die hard.

"I'm happy to answer any questions you have," Narinder says, her voice full of compassion.

Mum doesn't answer at first; she's touching Leo's face. "He's so warm." Her hand travels down to rest upon the sheet. "I can feel his heart."

The unspoken question hangs in the air; how can he be so alive and still be dead? Schrödinger's Cat. Mr Archer nods. "We're able to keep it beating for quite some time."

There's an implication behind those words: they can but they won't. These machines will be needed for someone else soon, someone who might have a chance of recovery. Not Leo. And even though we've talked about this and I know there's no hope, a tiny part of me still struggles to accept it.

"How do you know he's not still in there?" I burst out. "I heard about this thing called locked-in syndrome, where the person can see and hear everything but can't communicate. Maybe that's what Leo has."

Mr Archer tilts his head. "Brain death isn't a diagnosis

we make lightly. Both myself and another senior doctor have assessed Leo and we are certain that Leo has gone. I'm very sorry."

"But how can you be sure?"

"Niamh," Mum murmurs. "Please. Let it go."

The anguish behind her words silences me. My hands clench and unclench at my sides and I think I might actually throw up. Then she looks at me and it's like she sees me for the first time since Leo fell. Her eyes widen and suddenly her arms are around me and she's clutching me so hard I can hardly breathe. I know she's crying, but only because she's shaking, not because she's making any noise. Dad steps forward, gathers us in his arms.

"How long...?" he begins, speaking over our heads, before trailing off and ending on a painful-sounding swallow.

"There's no rush," Narinder replies quietly. "There are some non-intrusive tests and tasks to be done. But you can take as long as you need with Leo."

The next few hours are the shortest and yet the longest I've ever known. Mum sits at Leo's bedside, his hand clasped in hers as she talks to him, reminiscing mostly about when we were small. I try not to listen – it's hard hearing her voice catch, seeing fresh tears trickle down her cheeks. And in the back of my mind there's the nagging reminder that Leo has always been her favourite.

She'd never admit it, not even to Dad, but why wouldn't he be? Leo wasn't hormonal and moody; he didn't get angry and cry for no reason, or get excluded for telling a teacher to do one. Up until yesterday, Leo had always been a parent's dream, whereas I – well, I've only ever been a disappointment.

As the minutes and the hours pass, I wonder if deep down, she's expecting him to wake up. But I realize she's not talking to him, not really. She's remembering, fixing things in her mind so that her last memories of him aren't only of how he is now, inert and unresponsive. She's letting go, a little bit at a time.

Dad finds it harder to talk to Leo. His voice cracks when he tries and he presses his lips together and stares at the wall. And I can't speak at all. I look at Leo, oblivious to our pain, and imagine him stiff and cold. The thought makes it hard to breathe.

Hospital staff come in and out, always with bowed heads and kind eyes as they change drips, check monitors, take blood, respectful and gentle. They help us take Leo's handprints too, which someday will hang next to the tiny ones from our nursery days. And Mum thanks every single person.

Narinder comes in to check on us from time to time but I never get the sense she's hurrying us, more that she gets how hard this is and wants to help if she can. The last time she comes in, we're silent. And even though Mum is still holding Leo's hand, there's a difference in the way she's sitting; a sense of calmness that wasn't there before.

"Is there anything you need?" Narinder asks.

Mum blinks, as though she's forgotten who Narinder is. She lets out a long shaky breath and her eyes seek Dad's. There's no need to speak – I know what she's asking. Tears roll down Dad's cheeks as he manages a single nod. Then Mum is looking at me. My gaze flickers to Leo, peaceful and unnaturally still. Somehow, I nod too.

Mum shuts her eyes for a second then turns to Narinder. "I think...I think we're ready."

The nurse's eyes glitter with sympathy. "You're sure?"

Dad glances at Leo and for a moment I think he's going to change his mind. Then he lets out a broken sigh. "Yes."

The room fills with people then; more nurses, Mr Archer, and another doctor I don't recognize. Narinder stays, exchanging medical terms with the rest of the team and explaining to us what's happening. Not that we need much explanation – the ever slowing blip of the heart monitor tells us everything we need to know. And then finally there's just a flat line and Mr Archer looks at us with sad eyes.

"He's gone," he says, his voice soft but clear. "I am so very sorry."

I think I might burst with the effort of keeping it together as we leave Leo for the last time. I can't take my eyes off him, can't process the knowledge that this is the last time I'll see him. Dad kisses his forehead, too choked up to speak. Mum smoothes his hair, her eyes lingering on his pale, peace-filled face. Then she takes my hand and squeezes it tight.

"It's not goodbye," she whispers. "Not really."

Dad takes her other hand and somehow, we walk out of the room.

E m and I are playing poker mid-morning when the news comes. At least, I'm playing poker – Em is shuffling her cards around and frowning a lot. It's just as well I like her or she'd owe me a lot more than three Snickers bars and a crappy boy band CD. Then suddenly Mr Bartosinski is standing beside the curtains, my parents just behind him. "I've got some news, Jonny."

Em starts to get up.

"Don't go," I say, filled with uneasiness. "She can stay, can't she?"

My consultant dips his head. "If that's what you want."

At first I think I'm imagining it when he says there's a heart. I mean, I've fantasized about it so many times –

visualization, the psychologist calls it, the idea you can make something happen just by thinking about it. If that was true, all of us sick kids would get better. But Mr Bartosinski doesn't crack a grin and tell me he's messing with my head. He simply stands there, waiting for my reaction, and slowly it dawns on me that he's for real. My parents don't seem surprised, making me wonder if they already knew, although Dad still stutters when he asks if they're sure. Mr Bartosinski nods: the heart has been assessed by the surgical team, they're happy it's a match. And I suddenly understand why Femi skipped me at breakfast – he must have known this was coming. "Special plans for you, Jonny," he'd called, wheeling the trolley by. "Nil by mouth."

I'd thought he meant blood tests.

"We got the call in the early hours of this morning," Mr Bartosinski explains, as though reading my mind. "But we wanted to be sure it matched your very individual requirements before we said anything to you."

He glances at my parents, confirming my suspicion that they knew long before this. I try not to mind that they didn't tell me; does that mean there have been other hearts that haven't matched? What else haven't they told me?

Mr Bartosinski clears his throat. "Is there anything you want to ask?"

Is he kidding? There are around a million questions

crowding into my head. How long will it take? What if it doesn't work? I've heard stories about new hearts that didn't beat, couldn't cope, needed time. What if it makes things worse? Although it's hard to imagine being worse off than I am now, besides being in a coffin. Emily squeezes my hand and from the look on her face she's guessed what's going through my head. My parents are practically waving pom-poms, determined to look on the bright side, the way they have been from the moment they realized their baby wasn't normal, but Em knows what it's like to be terrified of the gathering dark.

"Will...will it feel any different?" I croak, my throat suddenly sandpaper-dry. "The heart, I mean. Will I be able to tell it's...not mine?"

The moment the words leave my lips, I go hot with embarrassment. What am I asking – whether I'll get somebody else's feelings? It sounds ridiculous even to me. But Mr Bartosinski doesn't laugh. "No," he says, as though I've asked something perfectly reasonable. "Think of it as swapping out a faulty fuel pump in a car. The car runs better once the fuel supply is improved but it doesn't understand why."

I tip my head to one side. "Except it's not as simple as that, is it? In a car, the rest of the engine doesn't attack the new pump."

Mr Bartosinski nods. "The body will try to reject the

transplanted heart. You'll need to take medicines every day for the rest of your life to fool your body into accepting it. But that's something your transplant coordinator, Nick, can prepare you for." Mr Bartosinski is watching me, eyebrows raised. "If you want to go ahead with the operation, that is…"

This is it, the moment I've been waiting for. I stare down at the red liquid coursing through the tubes across my chest, listen to the quiet hum of the pump as it keeps me alive and I can't help thinking about the heart I'm about to get. Maybe as recently as yesterday it was part of someone else, pumping their blood so effortlessly that I bet they hardly even noticed it was there. It freaks me out a bit. "Whose heart was it?"

"You know I can't tell you that, Jonny," Mr Bartosinski says calmly. "It's best that you don't know. Although our specialist team can pass along a thank-you letter at some point, if you and the donor's family decide that's what you want."

"I want to know," I insist, though I'm not sure why it matters. "How old were they?"

He stares at me for several long seconds. "Someone not much older than you. A male. That's all I'm allowed to say."

Someone not much older than you… The words make me feel sick. A boy – not like me, because if he was like me I wouldn't be getting his heart – but someone who'd barely lived at all. I wish I hadn't asked.

"Don't think about it now, love," Mum says, frowning at the look on my face. "It's natural that you're curious but we can think about all that later."

There's such pleading in her eyes. I shouldn't be surprised she wants to get on with it – this is what we've been hoping for after all, as we've watched the other cardiac kids come and go. And maybe I'm being morbid by thinking of the boy who died, though I don't see how I can ignore him. Did he know he was dying? Or was it an instant thing, the essence of life snuffed out, leaving only the body behind? I glance at Emily, who is watching me with a weird expression. It takes me a minute to work out that it's envy I can read in her eyes, although she's trying her hardest to hide it. I can't say I blame her. I suppose it does seem like I'm getting a miracle cure: if this operation goes well I'll almost certainly be fixed, whereas she has plenty of puke-inducing treatment left with no guarantees at the end. That's when I realize I should stop dicking around and take the heart.

"Do it," I say, trying to stop my voice from wobbling. "Please."

"Okay," Mr Bartosinski says. "Things will move very fast from now on – you'll go to theatre in about fifteen minutes and the surgical team will start the procedure in an hour. Nick will be with you for as long as possible, to answer any further questions."

Dad gnaws at a fingernail. "How long before you'll be able to let us know how he's doing?"

"Even the most straightforward heart transplants take between four and six hours," Mr Bartosinski replies, making me wince. "But by the halfway point we should have an idea of how things are going. Someone will update you then."

He looks at me, his gaze measuring and reassuring at the same time. "This has been a long time coming, hasn't it, Jonny?"

He can say that again: fourteen years to be precise and he's been there every step of the way. And now that we're here, I'm scared it won't fix me at all. Sometimes, patients die in surgery or after the operation. But the truth is, I don't have much of a choice – it's this or play Russian roulette with the blood clots. When I look at it like that, it's simple.

"Yeah, it has," I say, swallowing hard and trying to pull together the tattered strands of my pride. I push my poker winnings back towards Em. "Looks like you got lucky."

Her eyes glint as she stares back at me. "No. You did."

9

NIAMH

The sun comes up as we drive back to the cottage.

We don't talk much. The idea is that we'll pack fast and get away – none of us can face the thought of being here, with the endless stream of what ifs battering us, although the thought of going home without Leo feels even more unreal. Mum makes tea and toast that taste of nothing and we stand in the kitchen, staring into space, exhausted into silence. After a while, Dad puts his mug in the sink and manages the ghost of a smile. "We'd better get on."

I want to help, I really do. But Leo's breakfast bowl catches me out; it sits on the round kitchen table, the two lonely Cheerios in the bottom staring at me like weirdly spaced eyes. His half-drunk orange juice is abandoned beside it, reminding me how enthusiastic he was about visiting the beach and how it made me more determined to hate it.

"Don't worry, Niamh," he grinned, when he saw me scowling furiously at him, "fresh air isn't actually fatal to dorks."

I flicked him the V-sign then. He thought that was funny too.

I don't know how long I'm standing there before Dad comes in. I don't even know he's beside me until he gently pries the glass from my hand and mops up the spilled juice. "I'll sort this out. Why don't you go and pack your things?"

For the first time in for ever, I do as I'm told. I drop my lifeless phone on the bed. It's never been off this long but I don't want to charge it up, don't want to see everyone doing the stuff they always do, being normal. And it sounds stupid but I don't want people to find out about Leo – when they know, they'll intrude. Their sadness will be added to ours and I'm afraid it might suffocate us. Right now it's just us and it feels...controllable.

Next to my bed there's a stone I picked up on the beach. It's bleached white, smooth and almost round. In the centre, there's a perfect hole, worn away by time and the tide. I remember thinking when I found it that the stone was me, incomplete, damaged. Except now I know what it's really like to have a hole punched through your heart. We all do.

I find Mum sat on the bed in Leo's room, holding his sweatshirt to her chest, face buried in the material, breathing in his smell. The sight of her makes my stomach lurch. She looks so sad, so heartbroken. "Need any help?" I say, because I can't think of anything else.

She lets out a long shuddering sigh and nods, lowering the jumper. "Can you put his guitar away and take it to the car?"

The memory hits me hard – Leo standing at the base of the rocks, the certainty on his face as I demanded his guitar if I won. He was so sure he couldn't lose and I'd wanted to show him, for once, that he wasn't infallible. That stupid guitar. If it hadn't been for the flicker of possessiveness in Leo's eyes when I mentioned it, I might have refused to climb.

It's leaning against the wall, the protective nylon bag in a crumpled heap on the floor beside it. I want more than anything to smash it into the ground, break it into tiny pieces and grind them into the chintzy carpet. But I slip it into the bag and carry it downstairs, screaming in my head the entire time.

Eventually, we're done and we start the long drive home. I watch the cottage vanish in the rear-view mirror, see Mum's shoulders silently shaking and Dad's hands gripping the steering wheel so hard that his knuckles are white. Beside me, the seat is empty.

10

JONNY

My name is Jonny and I'm no longer a robot.

Don't get me wrong, I still sometimes have more wires than an Xbox but the mechanical part of me is gone. Instead, I have someone else's heart keeping me alive, lines of neat stitches and a scar to make sure I never forget it. I'm not Iron Man. I'm Frankenstein's monster.

It takes two weeks for them to let me out of the ICU. At first they had machines to breathe for me and to pump the blood around, so that my new heart could take it easy. It's all a bit hazy; I mean, I remember waking up and hearing the noise of the ventilator, and I remember trying to speak and my throat not working properly because of all the tubes they'd shoved down it. And I remember being afraid to move, even the slightest little bit, in case I split my stitches open. But those memories are vague and dreamlike. It's only the absence of the Berlin Heart that proves it was real.

I turn fifteen the day after I leave the ICU. My parents throw a little party, with a cake I can't eat and candles I just about manage to blow out. Femi comes along, even though it's his day off, and gives me an imported comic fresh from America. Em gets me a present too – a new sketchbook and some pencils – and makes me promise to draw her something soon. It's not exactly rock and roll – two sick kids, their nurse and a couple of old people. But it's been touch and go for a while whether I'd make this birthday so, believe me, I'm partying hard on the inside.

I still can't believe I'm off the machines. It's good to press two fingers into my wrist and feel the strong thud of this new heart as it does its job. I look better too – okay, I'll never be Hulk or Captain America, but it's amazing what a difference this new body part makes. In some ways, I'm kind of scared – I've been ill for so long that I'm not really sure what happens next. I'm not a robot. I'm not the boy with the death sentence. Now I'm just Jonny, taking twelve different drugs three times a day, with a badass scar and a stranger's heart beating in my chest. Thinking about that takes a bit of getting used to – someone not much older than me, Mr Bartosinski said. I wonder who he was, what he was into. And at the same time, I try not to think about that stuff because I'm not allowed to know the answers.

Whoever he was, I owe him.

In fact, I owe him everything.

11

NIAMH

The funeral is hard. Everyone tries to act like we're celebrating Leo – the vicar goes on and on about how he lit up so many lives, like scoring a few goals and pretending to be Kurt Cobain somehow made the world a better place. And people don't know whether to smile or sob. It doesn't help that I am dressed in a ridiculous yellow dress that makes me look like a Teletubby – my mother has banned us all from wearing black. But the worst part of it all is the fakery – girls from school in too-short skirts and trowelled-on make-up acting like they've lost their best friend when really Leo just smiled at them once. The boys don't bother me so much; at least they actually knew Leo. Watching them approach my mum and dad, mumbling indistinct apologies, might be funny if I felt capable of laughing. But the girls…they make me want to stab something.

"You look angry," my best mate, Helen, says as she hands me a glass of Coke and a plate piled high with curled-up sandwiches and stale Pringles from the buffet.

"I am angry," I reply, skewering a cocktail sausage on the plastic fork. "I'm the difficult one, remember – people expect me to be raging."

Helen raises an eyebrow. "But not murderous," she says, taking the plastic knife off my plate. "Those poor girls have suffered enough."

Her gaze skips to the fake mourners, flicking their hair by the salad bowls.

"Huh," I say, scowling. "Misery tourists."

There have been plenty of them, actually; a constant stream of distant family and friends have dropped by the house, bearing food and sympathy cards, reminding us that Leo is dead, in case we forgot.

There are some who've stayed away – Dad says it's not their fault, they don't know what to say. Then there are the online messages from kids at school I've never spoken to in my life: *So shocked about the accident. Thinking of u. Miss Leo so much.* His Facebook page is like a shrine, where the girls punctuate every comment with sad face icons and the boys swap gruff stories about how great he was. I don't know why I hate them so much – everyone loved Leo. But I don't recognize half these people; it doesn't feel like they have a right to be here.

"Aren't they Sophie's friends?" Helen asks.

Sophie was Leo's on-off girlfriend, all hair extensions and fake eyelashes. She's been round to visit too, quivering like a damp-eyed Disney princess. She tried to give me a hug in the hallway but I folded my arms at the last second so it was all one-sided and awkward. "Probably. They seem like her type."

"They do," Helen agrees. She glances around again. "How are your parents coping?"

I stare at my mother, dressed in emerald green that makes her hair seem redder than ever. She's smiling too brightly at something Great-aunt Milly is saying. Dad is with Leo's football coach, glassy-eyed but trying to look interested. "All right, I guess. They got a letter from the hospital a few days ago, telling us everything they took."

Helen looks uncomfortable. "It's weird, thinking that bits of him are still out there, *working*. I'm not sure I'd want that, if anything ever happened to me."

"It's what he wanted," I say, prodding at the egg and cress triangle on my plate. I try my hardest to sound indifferent but I have to admit I've thought about it a lot in the days since the accident: Leo's heart, still beating without him. I hope they gave it to someone decent, someone who gets how hard it was to let go.

We stand there in silence for a minute then Helen clears her throat. "You know it's results day next week?"

Of course I do – we're supposed to go into school to collect the results for the GCSEs we sat a year early. Leo was looking forward to his – two A*s were practically a formality – and I couldn't care less about my crappy statistics grade. I don't want to go back to school in September, don't care about my future. I just want to be left alone. "They're posting ours," I tell her. "Waste of a stamp if you ask me."

"I'll get mine posted too and then come see you on Friday, if you like," Helen says. "We can open them together."

"That sounds like a lovely idea, Helen," my mother says, from somewhere behind us. "We'll have a little celebration, just the…just us."

I roll my eyes at Helen. It won't be a celebration; it can't be. It will be miserable and awful. "Don't."

She smiles back. "Great. See you about nine-thirty, then?"

I know what my mother is thinking – if Helen comes round, I can't stay in bed. "Fine," I mutter, stabbing another cocktail sausage. "Don't expect me to get dressed."

12

JONNY

Em is in a bad way when I go to say goodbye. She's lying in her bed, eyes closed, pale-faced and puffy from all the steroids they're pumping into her. She's at stage three of the treatment for her kind of leukaemia, hopefully the last one, where they nuke the fluids in her brain and spinal cord with a mother lode of chemotherapy. It's pretty intense. Another time I'd prepare a joke about her hamster cheeks for when she wakes up but I don't really feel like joking around. Not today.

I sit at her bedside, working out what I'm going to say. It feels wrong somehow to be going home, like I'm abandoning her, even though we've known for weeks this day was coming. I'll still see her, of course – she's my Unbucket buddy – but I won't be just along the corridor with the other cardiac kids. And I won't be sick any more.

The poison in the bag hanging over Em's head is almost empty by the time she blinks at me. Her eyes are red and sore-looking, with heavy purple bruises underneath. Chemo might be a necessary evil but there's no denying it's a bitch.

"Hi," I say cheerfully. "You look like crap."

Her cracked lips twitch into an almost-smile. "I feel like it. You look so healthy it hurts. I hate you."

She says it without any bitterness. And the truth is, I feel good – not like I can prevent earthquakes or swallow nuclear bombs, but I can breathe and walk without gasping. Hospital kids are at the mercy of their numbers – white blood cells, red blood cells, platelet count, oxygen, the numbers are endless – and thanks to my mystery donor mine are getting better every day. I wish I knew more about him, even just his name, something to hang my thankfulness on, especially when I see how awful Em looks.

"Don't envy me too much," I tell her. "My parents have organized a big family party for me – balloons, hats and the kind of DJ who thinks ABBA are still a thing." I roll my eyes but Em's expression is wistful and I know she'd love to be sitting where I am, dorky party or no dorky party. "It will be your turn soon. Not long now."

She swallows and glances away. "Maybe."

"It will," I insist. "Look, you're Chemo-Girl, nemesis of cell mutations everywhere and saviour of mankind."

I hold up the drawing I've done for her, showing Em with electric-blue hair and bodysuit to match, zapping beams of jagged light at a blobby pink monstrosity with mean little eyes and a gaping mouth. She stares at it for the longest time, making me wonder if I should have drawn her boobs a bit smaller, then she smiles wearily. "That's pretty cool."

Getting to my feet, I walk round to the tall cupboard where she keeps all her stuff. "I'll stick it on the side of this, so you can see it every day."

The wood is already covered with cards from her friends, and a poster of her latest actor crush, but I clear a space, taking more pleasure than I should from sticking a blob of Blu-Tack right over his smug grin. That's when I realize Em has drifted off again – she'd never let me do that if she was awake.

I watch her sleep for a minute, reluctant to go without saying goodbye. But it's not like I'll never be back; I've got weekly check-ups to make sure my numbers are still on track and appointments with the transplant team counsellor to keep every other week – getting a new body part can be tough emotionally as well as physically so the hospital likes to make sure you're coping, inside and out.

All of which means I'll be able to hang out with Em plenty over the weeks ahead. But right now Dad is hovering by the door, pointing at his watch and doing a hopeful thumbs-up gesture. So I take Em's hand and squeeze her bony fingers ever so gently.

"See you later, Chemo-Girl. Message me whenever you want. And keep fighting."

If we were in a movie, she'd squeeze back. But she doesn't respond, shows no sign she's even heard. So I lay her hand on the bed again and go join my parents, who are waiting to do something they must have thought might never happen: take me home.

13

NIAMH

"Niamh?"

My mother's voice is as tentative as her knock on my bedroom door. I know what she wants, heard the doorbell go and Helen's cheerful greeting. I know too that the postman has been, because next door's dog went mental when he walked up the path, the way it does every morning. It hates the postman with every fibre in its scruffy little body. Today, I know exactly how it feels.

I'm about to turn over and face the wall when I hear the door handle start to turn. We have an agreement, my family and I – my bedroom is like a foreign country; they can't cross the border without my express permission. Opening the door is a declaration of war. Or it was, before Leo died. A lot of boundaries have shifted in the last four weeks.

"Helen's here." Mum's voice is louder now, telling me she's in the room. I keep my eyes closed. She comes nearer, steps on an empty crisp packet and hesitates. "Are you awake, Niamh?"

I'm in bed, my eyes are closed and I'm not responding – surely that's enough evidence to suggest that I am actually asleep? But there's a critical flaw in my thinking; my mother has just buried one of her children and she's terrified of losing the only one she has left. So when I lie perfectly still under the covers and don't reply, she feels compelled to make sure I'm still breathing. There's a whisper of wind as she holds a hand in front of my mouth. Her fingers accidentally brush my face.

The cool, rose-scented touch makes me twitch and the pretence is over. "Sorry," she says, as I open my eyes to glower at her. "But I'm sure you'd rather Helen didn't come up here." She glances around and I can tell she's resisting the urge to comment on the litter of clothes and rubbish covering the floor.

Yanking the duvet over my head, I shut my eyes again. "Tell her to go home."

There's a long silence. It's so long that I actually begin to wonder if she's taken me at my word and gone to get rid of Helen. But then I hear it, a muffled sob catching in the back of her throat, and I know she's crying.

I poke my head out of the crumpled duvet. "Mum,"

I say, as she blinks hard several times. "Don't cry. I'll get up."

She doesn't answer, just stares at the floor, her lips white from the pressure of keeping the pain from bursting the dam, tears lacing her eyelashes. When she does speak, her voice is small and lost.

"I put Leo's letter away, so that Dad and I could open it together when he gets home from work, but every time I looked at your envelope, I saw his name. I had to hide yours too."

I don't know what to say. There's been so much of this – our lives are unsurprisingly still full of Leo, as though he's gone away for a little while but will be back any minute. Mum and Dad can't bear to throw anything of his away, so there are three issues of *Kerrang!* lying unopened on the hall table, a list of dates he's meant to play football pinned to the fridge, the note he stuck to the last Mars bar in the cupboard warning me he'd kill me if I ate it. He's everywhere. No wonder she sees his name instead of mine.

"We can open ours somewhere else if you like," I say, sitting up and pulling yesterday's jumper over my head, "go to McDonald's. Helen's always up for a Sausage & Egg McMuffin."

I predict Mum's answer even before she starts to shake her head. Aside from letting me take my refuge in my room, she's hardly let me out of her sight since the funeral, clucking around like an anxious hen after a midnight raid by the foxes. I think she just needs to know where I am. All. The. Time.

"No," she says, making a visible effort to pull herself together. "I want to know how you did."

I don't. Squiggles on a bit of paper, that's all this result is to me. There's talk of sending me to a counsellor once a week to help me with "the grieving process" – I bet they'd love to dissect my reluctance to go back to school – spout some rubbish about it being a natural reaction to avoid a place that reminds me so much of Leo, and how his death holds up a mirror to my own mortality. But it's not that – well, not totally. I don't mind talking about the present but if I try to think of what I'll be doing even a month from now, everything goes dark. I don't trust the future; it wants to swallow me up. But now is okay. Now is safe.

Mum is watching me, her face pinched with anxiety, and I have a sudden flashback to that day on the beach, when she looked at me the same way, willing me to play happy families, make an effort with Leo, not be such a psycho-bitch. A lump swells in my throat. Look where that got us.

Standing up, I reach for yesterday's jeans. "Let's get it over with."

Downstairs, Helen is sitting on the edge of the sofa, staring at the sympathy cards covering every surface. What's the etiquette with them? How long do you leave them up for after you've read them so often you know all the messages by heart? And then what do you do once you've taken them down – put them out with the recycling or keep them as a reminder of what you've lost?

Helen is holding her own envelope from school with both hands, like it might bolt if she loosens her grip. She smiles when she sees me but I know, underneath, she's nervous.

"Sorry to make you get dressed," she says, looking up at me with a grin that tells me she's not in the least bit sorry. "I would have come up but I hear your room is a biohazard."

"Don't believe everything the bedroom police say," I reply. "They've got their own agenda."

Mum smiles. If you didn't know her, you might be fooled into thinking she's holding it together pretty well. But I know she's not sleeping much because I hear her creep into Leo's room in the dead of night, when I'm lying awake. Dad is better but he's still got this vacant look in his eyes, one I've seen so often lately. Sometimes his gaze slides right through me like I'm not even there. Our house has become this Bermuda Triangle of Misery, with Leo's death a great big plane crash in the centre.

Helen waves her envelope at me. "Shall we?"

I look for my envelope – there's no sign of it. For one wild, irrational moment, I think Mum has imagined its arrival. Then she goes to the bookshelves, pulls out our battered copy of Leo's favourite childhood book, *Dear Zoo*, and opens it. Sandwiched between the pages are two white envelopes, the same as the one Helen is holding. Mum hands mine over, her fingers shaking, and I'm filled with the sudden urge to get away.

My stomach clenches. "Helen—"

"Let's swap," she interrupts, plucking my envelope from my hands and shoving her own into my now empty hand. "You open mine and I'll open yours."

And before I can stop her, she's tearing the flimsy paper and tugging the folded sheets out. After a moment, she looks up, her expression unreadable.

"Well?" I say, not sure I want to know the answer. "How bad is it?"

Helen nods at the envelope in my hand. "Open mine first."

I could refuse to play, hand the stiff oblong back to her and hide until she's given up on me. But Mum is watching and waiting, holding her breath, as fragile as a butterfly. And the need to get this over with wins. Ripping the envelope open, I pull out the paper inside.

The letters dance before my eyes, then line up properly and I see two perfect A* grades – one for statistics and one for music. I should be pleased for her, she's worked hard for them both. Instead I feel empty. Leo took music too.

"Niamh?" she says, holding out her hand with a weird

expression of anticipation and dread. "We swap on three, okay?"

I'm tempted to screw the paper up. Then I remind myself that this is Helen – my best friend – this matters to her. If I was any kind of decent human being, I'd smile and congratulate her.

I take a breath. "Okay."

My fingers grip the cool paper and we stare into each other's eyes. "One…two…three!"

Her gaze drops to her sheet and I see relief and elation cross her face. She looks up, glowing. "God, I thought I'd done all right but I didn't imagine this!"

I expect to have to force a smile but she looks so happy that when it comes, it's genuine. "Well done."

She grins back at me. "Well done, yourself."

Mum claps her hands together in delight and steps towards me – I'd almost forgotten she was there. I move back, jerking the paper up so she can't see it and trying to ignore her hurt look. Surely I'm entitled to read it myself first?

It's better than I deserve, considering how little revision I did: a solid B. Something wriggles and shifts inside me. It might be pride, satisfaction or even pleasure but it's gone before I can catch it. "Here," I say, holding the sheet towards my mother.

"Oh, Niamh," Mum says, and I can tell from the wobble in her voice that she's crying again. "Well done!"

And before I know it, Helen has launched herself at me and is hugging me. "Get off," I say, half laughing, half embarrassed. "Idiot."

Out of the corner of my eye, I see Mum is nearby. Maybe she's waiting for me to turn and hug her. But when I look at her properly, I see her eyes are fixed on *Dear Zoo*, lying closed on the table, the other white envelope sticking out of the top and the weight of Leo's absence flattens any glimmer of happiness I have.

"Mum?" I say and she drags her gaze reluctantly back to me.

"Let's go and celebrate," she says, dredging up a smile that goes nowhere near her eyes. "Sausage & Egg McMuffin, isn't it, Helen?"

Helen goes home after we've eaten, to share her results with her parents and celebrate her brilliance properly. Mum goes to bed as soon as we get home, pale and shaky with a migraine, leaving me to sit in our silent house. It was never this quiet when Leo was here – he was always clattering or banging about, practising guitar, shooting hoops in the garden, drawing attention to himself. He'd been that way for as long as I could remember: *Look at me, Mummy, look at me – I'm balancing. Look at my picture, Daddy, isn't it better than Niamh's? Look…look!*

I find it hard to settle, don't want to go back to bed so I take a walk to the chemist's, thinking I'll pick up Mum's antidepressant prescription and get some pills for her head. And on the way back, I take a couple of tablets myself. I'm not sure what I expect them to do – I don't think you can buy the kind of pills that stop you thinking over the counter in Boots.

The house feels even quieter when I get back. Leo's envelope is still on the table, poking out of *Dear Zoo*, and all of a sudden, I miss him. Not the noise he made, or his exuberance, or the arrogance, because they drove me out of my mind, but *him*. The part that was always my brother. And there's only one place I want to be.

His room is freakishly tidy. Seriously, it was never like this before. If I close my eyes, I can see the piles of clothes on the floor, the football kit strewn across the chair and hear Mum nagging him to put it in the washing machine. It doesn't smell right, either, no underlying scent of smelly feet masked by Lynx. Chelsea's star striker grins down at me from the wall and there's a corkboard with a revision timetable pinned to it. I almost smile then, because Leo always claimed his predicted grades were based on natural ability, not hard work and here's the proof he lied. Just like he lied about stealing my birthday money to spend on new guitar strings, denying it and denying it until eventually Mum took his side and I flew at him in a fury. It took both our parents to drag me off him and I refused to apologize, refused to speak to him for weeks, even when threatened with withdrawal of wi-fi. That's when Mum booked the holiday to Devon. She'd had enough, she said, of living in a war zone.

I perch on the bed, freshly made but with a small, head-shaped dent in the pillow, as though he was lying here a few moments ago. His guitar is in its stand. I remember carrying it to the car, wanting to smash it. I still feel a bit like that, to be honest. I don't want to miss Leo. I don't want to unconsciously listen for his size-ten feet thundering down the stairs each morning, better than any alarm clock. I don't want to wish that we'd never argued, that I'd been a better sister. And I don't want to carry this crushing guilt that I robbed the world of someone better, someone brighter than me. Everywhere I look, there's evidence of Leo's potential – the football trophies he won, the guitar he excelled at, the exam results downstairs. I curl up on the bed, closing my eyes against the hot pressure of tears I feel building. I'm tired of always being in his shadow. Even now he's dead, I can't break free.

The click of the door handle wakes me up. Dad is standing in the door frame, a pair of football boots in his hand and a startled expression on his face. "Niamh. I— What—?"

I can't quite meet his gaze. "I fell asleep," I mumble. My sleep-heavy eyes fix on the boots. "Are those Leo's?"

He hesitates, then nods. "Yes. I got the studs done, in case..." He lets out a shaky laugh. "I don't really know why. It just seemed like the right thing to do."

"Oh." I can't think of anything else to say. "Right."

He takes a few steps forward just as I sit up and push myself off the bed. There's an awkward moment when we're face to face and then I'm past him and he's staring down at the covers.

"Dad?" I say, stopping in the doorway, watching him straighten the duvet, shake out the pillow. I pause, waiting for him to look up, waiting for him to see me. I want to tell him I understand why he got Leo's boots fixed. But he doesn't look at me. Instead, he reaches down and presses softly on the pillowcase, recreating the head-shaped dent, the illusion that Leo has only just left. Then he picks up the boots and takes them to the wardrobe.

I don't think he notices me slip out. It's not until I'm back in my own room that I realize I still have Mum's antidepressants in my pocket. The packet bounces as I drop it onto my bedside table and tumbles down the gap beside the bed. I leave it where it falls and let myself drift off again.

14

JONNY

Halfway through September, I start going to college.

It's kind of like school but not. I mean, obviously there are some things that are the same, like lessons and teachers and barely edible food in the canteen, but we don't have to wear uniform and we get to call the teachers by their first names. We talked about me going back to my old school but just the thought of the curious and pitying stares made me feel sick. So my parents found somewhere new, the kind of place kids go to get some qualifications when they've missed a lot of school or can't deal with the whole "achieve or else" attitude some teachers have.

College has quite a different vibe to it – freer, more relaxed, like you're allowed to breathe and be yourself.

Which is ironic really, since I'm not totally sure who I am these days. Being in hospital shrinks your world; you try to stay positive and keep busy but eventually, it becomes an endless cycle of tests, treatments, trying not to die – basically, you become your illness. Towards the end, it felt like people looked at my notes more often than me.

If you're lucky like I was, you get well and they let you out. The trouble is then that your world is still small – I don't know whether the things I like are because I was so ill and couldn't do the normal, everyday stuff my mates took for granted. And if I'm being totally honest, being out of hospital is kind of overwhelming sometimes; it's been two months since my operation – weeks since I went home – and the nagging feeling that I don't know who I am has been growing all that time. The thought messes with my head a bit – I suppose this is how Captain America felt, when he was set free from his suspended animation to discover that he didn't fit in any more.

Part of me wants to draw a line under life before my transplant – give myself a fresh start. I've even shut down my old Facebook account and started a new one, to represent the new healthy me; Jonny 2.0 has a grand total of thirty-six friends and no liked pages. No drawings, either; that's something the old Jonny did when he was too ill to do much else and it brings back too many memories. My sketchbook is stuffed in my wardrobe, out of sight, until I can look at it without feeling like I'm in that hospital bed again.

Apart from drawing, I don't have any hobbies. I don't do sport, for obvious reasons, although the hospital have told me I can – *should* – try some non-contact sports now, whatever that means. There's always music, I suppose – there are a few bands I like, and a lot more I definitely don't, but there's nothing about me that says "I am Jonny Webb". Jonny 2.0 is a blank space, ready to be filled, which is exciting and terrifying at the same time; how often does anyone get the chance to create a brand-new version of themselves? Where do you even start?

Then there's the boy whose heart I got: I've been thinking about him a lot – who he was, what he was like. It's the freakiest thing to imagine it pumping inside someone else. The transplant team counsellor says it's natural to wonder about my donor but I'm pretty sure it's not natural to lie there at night listening to the rhythmic thuds and trying to picture your heart's previous owner as often as I do. I'm also fairly certain you're not supposed to hook up with your good friend Mr Google and try to find out his name.

Anyway, apart from a morbid obsession with my second-hand heart's origins, things are going okay. My GCSE classes haven't been too stressful so far – I'm quite concerned for that Hamlet dude's mental health, but the work isn't too hard. And I'm enjoying the little things that come with not being ill – running upstairs without getting dizzy, having an appetite, going out to college. Dad insists on dropping me outside the gates every morning, though he's let me walk home on my own twice now.

"All set?" Dad asks each day as he pulls up outside the entrance, trying hard to sound chilled out but not quite hitting the note. "Got your pills? Got your sunblock?"

And I smile and nod as I get out of the car. "Yeah. See you later, Dad."

I could do without wearing Factor 50 sunblock, if I'm honest, but there's nothing I can do about that – the drugs put me at greater risk of skin cancer and Em would kill me if I didn't cream up. It just reminds me that I'm different to all the other kids here.

Starting a few weeks late means I'm already an outsider. Sometimes, I miss the closeness in the hospital – there was always someone to talk to there, even if they were only three years old. And I miss Em. I see her when I go in for my check-ups, although they're less frequent now. We message each other too – keep up the banter – but I miss knowing she's just at the end of the corridor. I think Mum has guessed I'm a bit isolated; she made me meet up with a couple of old mates from school, which was awkward – it's been over a year since I was hospitalized and since I wasn't exactly a regular attender even before that, none of us knew what to say. They did their best, asked about my operation and wanted to see my scar but I could sense I wasn't one of them any more: Captain America, an outsider looking in. It's pretty much what convinced me I needed a fresh start. We agreed to keep in touch but…let's just say I didn't send out many friend requests from my new Facebook account.

Most of the kids at college are doing vocational stuff, childcare and media studies, or resits. I don't want anyone to ask about why I dropped out of school, don't want to tarnish this brand-new me with pitying glances, so I keep mostly to myself. I suppose I could make friends with the kids on my course, except that fifty per cent of them don't actually want to be there. Out of the other half, a few are high achievers who couldn't cope with the brutality of school, a couple have been ill and the rest seem like average kids trying to get by. One reckons his failure is a conspiracy cooked up by a teacher who hated him at his previous school. His name is Marco. He sits at the back of the class in an ancient leather jacket and ripped skinny black jeans, slouched in his seat and radiating attitude, daring the teachers to say something. There's something almost admirable about the way he clearly couldn't give a toss what anyone thinks. I wonder if Jonny 2.0 could learn a thing or two from him.

I never see him around outside of lessons, though, have

no idea where he goes in between classes – he's never in the social area. It's not until our ICT teacher pairs us up to work on a questionnaire together that I realize Marco knows my name. Sort of.

"All right, Jonno?" he says, fixing me with an arrogant black-eyed stare. I know two things instantly – one, that I'm not going to correct him and two, that it's obvious who is going to be doing all the work here. I don't mind that so much – like I said, I'm enjoying the little things, homework and all, but I do mind the unspoken assumption that I'm somehow his bitch.

"You know what, mate?" Marco says at the end of the lesson, when the teacher has praised the work we've produced. "You're not as much of a loser as I thought."

There's a tiny part of me that's pleased with this half-compliment. Maybe the new improved Jonny could use a bit of Marco's attitude.

15

NIAMH

"**R**oom B303," I mumble, staring at the timetable in my hand and wondering if there's been some kind of mix-up. I've been at this school for four years – how can there be rooms I've never heard of? It's not bloody Hogwarts.

It's my first day back. I cut across the memorial garden, trying to ignore the modest marble statue underneath a willow tree in the centre. Leo isn't the only one immortalized in here – there's the girl who died from anaphylactic shock the year we started school and the boy who drowned in Hyde Park in the nineties. But Leo's is still the name on everyone's lips, even three weeks into the term. I hear it follow me along the corridors, an insidious whisper winding around my head wherever I go. People stare at me too – it's like I've got a flashing arrow over my head, *TRAGIC TWIN*, making me feel I shouldn't have come back to school at all. No one knew who I was last year. Now everyone does.

Sophie plays the devastated girlfriend like a pro. I'm amazed she's not dressed from head to toe in black instead of school uniform, dabbing at her perfectly contoured cheeks with a tissue like she'll never get over the loss. You'd think Leo was the love of her life but the truth is they'd gone through more break-ups than Taylor Swift and he wasn't really serious about her. He liked the idea of a girlfriend, as long as it didn't get in the way of his football and music. Not that you'd know that from watching Sophie.

I hurry down the corridor, scowling at each door in turn. Finally, at the end of a corridor I'm sure I've never been down before, I see B303. The door is closed, a bad sign. For a moment, I think about turning around and walking back the way I've just come. No one would blame me – I'm grieving. In fact, I'll never have a better excuse to skive off. But then I see Leo's smile and think of how enthusiastic he was about starting Year Eleven and I know I can't walk away. Besides, it's English, my favourite subject. So I take a deep breath and push open the door.

Two things hit me instantly: the absence of the teacher

and the way the conversation stops the moment everyone sees me. Silence hangs in the air, then they start talking again: whispering. Heat burns in my cheeks and I almost throw up on the spot.

It's the sympathy that bothers me most. I can stand the curiosity, although the feel of all those eyes on me makes my skin itch. But the sympathetic expressions are unbearable. *Poor Niamh*, they say, *we know how you feel.*

They don't. They haven't watched their brother smash against the rocks, seen his eyes shut for the last time, had to stand by while his body was divided up and given away. They don't wake up each day wondering what they could have done differently.

Heart thudding so hard it hurts my eardrums, I fix my gaze on the floor and push my way to the back of the class. Every lesson will be like this, maybe for the whole year. I wish I'd listened to my gut and run. I wish I'd stayed in bed. But then I would have had to deal with Mum and her new-found obsession with fundraising.

She's got this idea that Leo's death will mean something if she can raise fifty grand for the air ambulance service that carried him to the hospital. It's all she talks about; Dad seems to be humouring her but I do my best to shut her out. I know having a goal is meant to help her to cut back on the antidepressants. But still – she could change the playlist once in a while.

"Niamh!" calls a voice to my left. I turn to see Precious Muamba staring at me, her brown eyes so wide they seem to take up her entire face, her lips twisted into a pitying grimace. "How are you, babe?"

Her fingers reach towards me and I realize with horror that she's going to take my hand. I open my mouth to fob her off but the door opens again, causing the words to die in my throat. It's not Mr Mushtaq, though. It's Sophie.

Instantly, Precious switches channel. I stare at her as she forgets me and hurries over to pour fake sympathy on Sophie instead.

I fix my gaze on my desk. Although I try to avoid Sophie, her appearance does me a favour right now because suddenly the focus is on her instead of me. Three boys actually get up to help her to her seat. And then someone whispers to Sophie. She turns and looks my way. Her eyes glisten as she stretches out a hand towards me. "Niamh."

I freeze inside, caught between anger and shame. She barely spoke to me when Leo was alive and now we're supposed to be – what? *Sisters?* And I'm meant to want that too, with a girl who would never have talked to me if it wasn't for Leo.

I'm not sure I can cope with a year of this. Actually, I can't even take an hour.

Snatching up my bag, I stumble to the door. And twenty-five pairs of eyes watch me leave.

16

JONNY

"**E**arth to Chemo-Girl. Come in, Chemo-Girl!"

Em looks startled when I burst dramatically through the gap in the curtains and skid to a halt beside her bed. I clasp my hands together and heave a grateful sigh. "Thank God, I've found you. There's a mutation rampaging down Regent Street and only you can stop it!"

She rolls her eyes and laughs. "Back again? It's like you can't keep away."

"Been for a review," I say, flopping into the chair next to the bed. "They pumped so much dye into my arteries I'm amazed I'm not glowing. But I got the all-clear."

Em nods and studies me, like she's one of the consultants looking for signs of a relapse. I already know she won't find any – I feel good, fitter than I've ever been. And I've practically moved into our fridge so there's actual flesh between my skin and bones. I can't eat everything, of course, a lot of food has too much salt and fat and other bad stuff, and the medication I'm on can cause weight gain, but one of these days I might risk a Big Mac. You only live once, right?

Em looks better too – the bruises have gone from under her eyes and her lips aren't cracked any more. Her nose is still red – I guess the hairs in her nose haven't grown back yet. There's downy fuzz covering her head, though, a dark chocolate brown that reminds me of how she looked when we first met. Back then, she had masses of tumbling curls that she claimed to hate because they were so hard to brush. And then they started to fall out and she cried for days. I'm glad her hair is coming back – it doesn't always, not with the kind of high-strength blasting she's had – although I can't help wishing it was Chemo-Girl blue.

Her hand flies to her head when I mention the regrowth, causing her tubes and lines to rattle against each other. "I keep forgetting it's growing again, it gives me a heart attack every time I look in the mirror." Her eyes stray to my chest and her mouth quirks into a half-smile. "No offence."

"None taken," I say easily, because heart problems are something that belong to the old Jonny, not the new, surgically-enhanced me. I point at her hair. "So does this mean what I think it means?"

"Not officially," she warns but I can tell from the sparkle in her eyes that it's good news. "You know what the consultants are like – they won't confirm anything yet. I'm not having any more treatment, though."

I have the strangest urge to hug her then, to sweep her into my arms and press my lips against her fuzzy head. That's another effect of being well, I've discovered – I'm noticing girls more. Although Em's not really a girl, she's a mate – which makes this feeling all the weirder. Pushing the thought away, I settle for a high five. "See?" I say, and put on my best movie trailer voice. "Emily Mitchell is Chemo-Girl!"

"Maybe," she says, glancing at the picture I drew for her. "Enough about me, anyway. Tell me what it's like on the outside."

Where to begin? I wonder. *And what to leave out?* I know Em thinks she wants to hear about how great it is to be out of hospital but I don't want to lay it on too thick. So I tell her about my mother messaging me twenty times a day to make sure I've taken my anti-rejection meds, and my dad worrying about me walking home from college when I'm pretty sure I could run and it wouldn't bother me. They weren't happy about me coming up to the wards today, worried about the germs I might pick up – even now,

96

I reckon they're sitting anxiously in the cafe, sipping tea and shredding napkins. I don't mention that to Em. Instead, I describe the kids in my class. "Some of them are on another planet," I say, picturing Marco as I speak. "One of them acts like he's on drugs."

"You're on drugs," Em points out, with a grin.

I shake my head. "I know mine give me mood swings but he takes it to the next level. He totally ignored me for ages, then all of a sudden he's calling me 'mate'. I can't work him out. And I think the teachers are scared of him."

"Sounds like someone to avoid," she says. "Don't you see any of your old mates?"

It's different for Em – she's kept in touch with her friends from school and has a steady stream of visitors, even though she's been sick for a long time now. I'm not sure how to explain that I don't want to see the mates I used to have – they remind me of not being able to breathe and feeling so tired I could barely open my eyes. Of not fitting in. Those aren't memories I want. I'd rather make new friends, ones who have no idea who I used to be. "Not much. It's hard when we're at different schools."

The look she fires my way suggests she sees right through me but she doesn't say so. "What else have you been up to?"

I hesitate for a second. Should I tell her what's been keeping me awake at nights? That I can't stop wondering about my donor? Or that I've started to search out teenage deaths around the time of my operation – believe me, my internet search history is a trail of tragedy that would make even Doctor Doom cry. Maybe I should tell her what I haven't admitted to anyone else – that my heart won't really feel like part of me until I know where it came from. And once I've got a name, I can understand who he was, what he liked, how he came to save me.

It's like an itch that stays long after the wound has healed – I can't help scratching it. And I don't suppose Em will get it, not totally, but she's got a better chance than my counsellor, who has no idea what it's like to live when you thought you were going to die, or how it feels to know you're only alive because someone else is dead. Once I know my donor's name, everything will fall into place. He'll become part of who I am now: Jonny 2.0.

"Promise you won't tell anyone..." I begin.

NIAMH

17

"Is your mum really going to abseil down the Shard?"
Helen asks as we stroll across Hampstead Heath after
school one chilly October day.

It's the most ridiculous question I've ever heard. At
least, it would be a ridiculous question in a normal person's
world. The Shard is eighty-seven floors high – you don't
just hook up a rope and wander down it. But nothing is
normal any more. Not content with monitoring my every
breath, my mother has gone overboard on the whole
fundraising thing, even joining Facebook so she could set
up a page. And now she's agreed to abseil down the biggest
bloody skyscraper in London. Other people organize quiz
nights; my mother plans to jump off a building.

"Apparently," I mumble, kicking at a nearby patch of grass. "She's organized this group and they're all going to do it together. If she wasn't so pleased with herself, I'd think it was a suicide attempt."

Helen wraps her coat around herself and glances sideways at me. "I'm sure it's pretty safe. They wouldn't be allowed to do it otherwise. And it'll raise a lot of money – people love that kind of thing."

"Thanks. Maybe we could put it towards her funeral."

She slumps onto a damp wooden bench and looks up at me. "I think it's great that she's trying to make something good come out of Leo's death. It shows she's moving on."

"It shows she's mental," I grumble but I know what Helen means. Ever since Mum got in touch with the air ambulance people, she's cut down on the antidepressants and started to look better. Not happier, because she still breaks down over the smallest things, but like she's got a purpose instead of floating around the house and watching over me as though I'm a toddler again. I still hear her crying in the night, though, when I'm lying there staring at the ceiling. My counsellor, Teresa, says wanting to help others is an important part of recovery.

"Think of it as your mother's way of making sense of Leo's death," she said, when I told her about Mum's plans for a fundraiser day in the school grounds in a few weeks' time. "Sometimes it helps people if they feel as though they are making a difference in some way, no matter how large or small. Do you see?"

I stared resentfully around her ultra-white office – probably designed to be calming but it came across as soulless and clinical. There was a hot-pink orchid on the window sill. Its brightness caught my eye, mostly because colours seemed dull and lifeless these days, like they were covered by a dingy grey veil.

I focused on the orchid while I answered Teresa's question. "Oh yeah, like running the bake-off stand is going to save the world. At least there'll be plenty of cakes I can eat."

Teresa changed tack. "Are you eating well?"

It depended what she meant by "well" – I haven't eaten the super-healthy stuff Mum tried to make me eat, that was for sure. It didn't taste of anything. Then again, nothing really did. "All right, I suppose. Sometimes I can't really be bothered with food."

She wrote something on her notepad. "You should try to overcome that. Eating little and often might help. How are you sleeping?"

I wasn't much: every night was punctuated by dreams – disjointed, troubling and always ending with the same dull crunch. I didn't tell Teresa that, though. I'd started playing a game with her – give as little information as I could during each of our meetings so that her notepad was as uncluttered by writing as possible at the end of the session.

She watched me then, the skin between her eyes creased into two matching lines. I'd taken too long to answer – that meant something, apparently, because she wrote on the notepad again. "Fine," I said, more loudly than I intended to. "Sleep is fine. I am fine. Everything is FINE."

And on one level it was true: on the outside, I was, mostly. It was only on the inside that I was struggling, which made me wonder if we were *all* putting on a front, pretending to be fine so that the people around us didn't worry.

More writing. It wasn't a high-scoring day for me and my game.

I'm so busy thinking about Teresa and her stupid questions that it takes me a moment to realize Helen has said something. "What?"

She rolls her eyes. "I said, did you watch that spy thing that was on TV last night? The one with that guy from Harry Potter in it?"

I frown. The TV was on, I remember watching it but I couldn't say what was on. Sometimes it's hard to concentrate – I'll be staring at the screen and realize I've got no idea who the characters are or what they've been doing for the last ten minutes. "I don't know," I say to Helen. "Was it any good?"

Helen is pressing her lips together, a sure sign she's

got something to say. Time to change the subject, I think, and cast around for a distraction. "I got a weird message on Facebook at the weekend."

It works. Her eyebrows lift. "Weird as in deposed African dictator trying to give you eight million dollars, or weird as in Olga from Russia wants to make kiss-kiss with you?"

"Weirder," I say, sitting down beside her. "It was from some boy I'd never heard of, no mutual friends or anything, asking about Leo."

She frowns. "What about Leo?"

"That's what was strange about it. At first, I thought it was someone from school who'd found Mum's fundraiser page but when I checked out his profile, I saw he was from St Albans. And he wanted to know about Leo."

There's a long silence. "Okay, that is weird and quite a bit creepy. What did you say?"

"I asked him why he wanted to know. He never replied so I forgot about it. Until today." I hold out my phone for her to see.

"Hi Niamh," she reads, "sorry for the long silence. I'm writing an article about your brother for school and needed a bit more info. I know I sound like an insensitive knob but it would really help if you could give me some details."

I shiver – the sun is going down, turning the bushes and trees around us into black monsters against the peach and grey sky. It's time to go but I want to know what Helen thinks first. "So. Harmless weirdo or tragedy-obsessed freak?"

Helen stabs at the screen and studies his profile picture. "Jonny Webb. Are you sure you don't know him? Someone Leo played at football, maybe? He looks around the same age as us, although he's pretty weedy."

I watch her investigate his profile. There's not much to see – I know, because I've already looked. "He's only got forty-three friends," I say. "Even I have more than that and I'm Miss Unpopular, although he shares a lot of Avengers memes, so that probably explains it."

"You're only unpopular because you hate everyone," she reminds me, scrolling a bit more. "He's got no photos with mates. And no history beyond this year."

Our eyes meet and I know we're thinking the same thing. "Catfish."

"Or worse," she grimaces. "Delete and block. Now."

I take my phone back, planning to do exactly that, but I glance at Jonny Webb's face before I do. It's a nice face – not gorgeous but not ugly either. Ordinary, boy-next-doorish. His smile is a bit lopsided, one eyebrow is raised, as though he knows a joke he's not sharing. I wonder if he knows his picture is being used by a possible paedophile. But there's no way to warn him, no way to find out who he really is.

"Goodbye, Jonny Webb, you weirdo," I say, blocking the account and standing up. "Come on, let's go and see if my mother plans to jump off anything else."

18

JONNY

There's something going on with Marco in business today. He doesn't say anything but every time I glance across at him, he's watching me.

"What?" I mouth but he doesn't respond, just keeps on staring.

Shrugging, I do my best to ignore him. Maybe I was nearer the mark than I thought when I described him to Em: maybe he *is* on drugs. I'm stuffing my books into my bag at the end of the lesson when he finally decides to explain himself.

"We got stuff to talk about."

"Now?" I say, glancing at the clock. "I've got maths next."

"Nah," he says, shaking his head with a mirthless smile. "Come with me."

Punctuality isn't a concept Marco is really familiar with – he turns up to lessons when he feels like it and it looks like he's decided it's an approach I'm going to take too, at least where my next maths lesson is concerned. Soon we're down the steps and in the corner of the college car park, where the rebels are pulling their poison packets out to light up, away from the designated smoking areas. So that's why he's never in the social area. I should have known.

The clouds of smoke are already thick by the time we get there. I try not to breathe in, imagining the toxic fumes snaking towards my lungs and into my bloodstream but the moment my body starts to scream for oxygen, I give in and gulp down a greedy mouthful of the stinking air. The panicky fluttering feeling subsides as I force myself to remember that it's okay, I'm not dying any more. Well, no more than anyone else, although I have to take a bit more care of myself.

Marco doesn't seem to notice. "This is Jonno," he says to the others. "The one I told you about."

Five appraising glances are fired my way. I hold my ground, trying not to worry what my new trainers and expensive jeans say about me. I'm not obsessed with my appearance – mirrors are something you tend to avoid when you look like Death – but I've put on weight since I left hospital and most of my clothes are new. Mum and Dad were keen to spend money, spoil me the way they'd never been able to before, they said, so my stuff is pretty nice. But looking around, I see plenty of labels on show – it's only Marco who's gone for the grunge look. And saying that, I don't suppose vintage leather jackets are cheap.

"So?" one of the boys says, his gaze flicking back to Marco. "What's he gonna get us?"

Get them? What's that supposed to mean? But Marco beats me to it. "Shut up, Eavis. I haven't asked him yet."

"Asked me what?" I say.

Marco studies me through heavy-lidded eyes. "You're a druggy," he says baldly. "I seen you had a load of pills in your bag last week. We want to know if you're a pusher or a user."

I let out a short incredulous laugh. He means my medication, all neatly sorted into doses in labelled compartments so I know what to take and when. How many dealers are that organized? "Seriously, Marco, do I look like I sell drugs?"

He shrugs. "They come in all shapes and sizes. So you're a user then." He pauses to light up a cigarette. "What are you on?"

"What am I on?" I say, beginning to seriously wonder if I should be asking him the same question. "How long have you got?"

"We got all day," Marco says. "Maths can wait."

"It's medicine," I say, trying not to grit my teeth. I don't want everyone to know about my operation. They'll treat me differently once they know. "Prescribed by a doctor. Not the kind of stuff you buy under bridges."

One of the other boys – Billy, I think – shifts uneasily. "You never told us he's a sick note. What if it's catching?"

"You don't look sick," Marco replies, staring at me. "What's the matter with you?"

This is it, I think, the moment when everything changes. Once people know about my heart, they'll either treat me like I'm some kind of freak or avoid me, the way the kids at school did when I started to get ill. The scar would get a certain amount of horrified respect, if I decided to show it, but I don't want to be defined by my illness any more. That's who I used to be. Jonny 2.0 is better than that.

So I lie. "Ventricular tachycardia," I say, choosing something serious but treatable. "My heart sometimes beats really fast. The drugs help to control it."

It's not the way they treat long-term tachycardia – if it's severe enough you get a defibrillator stitched under your skin to sort out the electrical impulses in your heart – but these morons won't know that.

The one called Charlie frowns. "Isn't that what that footballer had? The one that collapsed in the middle of a match a few years back?"

He's not far wrong. I'm impressed in spite of myself. "No, he had ventricular fibrillation, which made his heart stop. Similar but different."

There's a silence. They are looking at me differently now, but it isn't revulsion I can see in their eyes – it's something like respect. Slowly, it dawns on me why. They admire footballers, including the one who died for seventy-eight minutes during a match, and some of that admiration has rubbed off on me, simply because they think we have the same medical condition. Wow. How stupid are this lot?

"Are the drugs you take any good?" one of them says, clearly determined not to get sidetracked. "Do they get you high?"

I think of the twelve different medicines I swallow every day. They do a lot of things; stop my body from rejecting my alien heart, make me gain weight and plenty of other stuff I can't even imagine, but they do not make me trip out. And it occurs to me that Marco and his mates are putting on an act – they don't know much about drugs at all. "No," I reply firmly. "And if you took them when you didn't need to, they'd put you in hospital."

Marco drops his cigarette to the floor and grinds the butt into the ground with his heel. "So basically, you're no use at all."

He looks bored rather than angry so I risk a grin.

"Apparently not. Unless one of you has an undiagnosed heart condition you need treatment for?"

He stares at me, then flicks his fingers towards the building. "Go on, then, back to school like a good boy."

I don't need to be told twice. Hurrying back into college, I hope the smell of smoke is gone by the time I head home. The last thing I need is an interrogation from my mother to round my day off.

Mum and Dad drag me out for a family dinner I've forgotten about, a celebration of my aunt's birthday with assorted relatives. I laugh politely when I'm supposed to, fidget through my low-fat main course, put up with their nosiness about my health and feel guilty when my cousins aren't allowed a dessert because I can't have one. And the moment we get home, I hurry up to my room with my laptop, all set to carry on trawling the internet for my donor. He has to have died less than three hours' distance from me at the hospital in London. Any longer than that and the organs don't make it. There have been one or two false alarms but the only match I've found so far is this kid Leo, who died on holiday with his family, poor sod. There's a Facebook page set up in his memory to raise money for the local air ambulance and I wouldn't mind if he was my donor – he looks like he had a decent life, plenty of mates and pictures of him winning football trophies. Good-looking too – there's a few of him with his arm around the same blonde, pretty but in a fake way; too much make-up. Why do girls do that, plaster their faces with crap and stick on eyelashes so big they could double as wind farms? Anyway, I reckon Leo had his pick of the girls. What I can't tell is whether he was an organ donor.

Em thinks I should leave it. Nothing good can come of knowing, she says, and she's probably right. I haven't told her I tracked down Leo's sister, invented some excuse to ask about his death. She looks younger than him in her profile pic; cute heart-shaped face and hardly any make-up. She's also allergic to smiling, as far as I can tell from the few pics I can see, although I don't suppose she has much reason to these days. I can't find her profile now so it looks like she's blocked me. I don't blame her – I'd do the same if I was in her shoes.

I can't help wondering, all the same. What if it *is* Leo's heart inside me? Would his family want to know who it went to? Or am I selfish to even think about it?

Em's right.

I should stop now before I get myself into trouble.

19

NIAMH

I watched this old movie called *Grease* once, where they transformed the high-school grounds into a graduation funfair at the end, so that Sandy and Danny could ride off into the clouds. If that scene had been set in a north London secondary school on an overcast Saturday in the middle of October, it would look pretty much like my mother's fundraiser day.

Oh, and there are posters of Leo dotted around, which are supposed to make us think he's with us in spirit. My mum is wearing a T-shirt with his face on, which I point-blank refuse to do because even in death, Leo's ego doesn't need feeding. I can't wear T-shirts now anyway – I've got Godzilla skin on my elbows that the doctor called stress-induced psoriasis. As if my life wasn't crappy enough.

Helen and I are running the cake stall and Helen has already eaten three slices of the rocky road someone donated. I feel a bit strange about eating something when I don't know who made it but Helen says that's how the entire food industry works and I should get over it. I'm not hungry anyway; I know it's all for charity but it makes me feel a bit sick. Practically the entire school has turned out in memory of my brother and I can't help wondering if they're smiling their fake smiles to my face, while whispering behind my back, *Why couldn't she have been the one who died?*

"I'm going to get a drink," Helen says, licking the last crumbs of cake from her fingers. "Want one?"

I shake my head and she disappears into the throng, leaving me on my own. There are too many people here. I know that's the idea, and I'm glad for my mum's sake, but the noise and the crowd is getting on my nerves. At least I don't have to worry about bumping into Sophie – she's on the other side of the field, selling balloons for the race later on. She's been round our house a lot in the last few weeks, helping Mum with the planning. Mum loves her – I'm pretty sure she's the daughter my mother would have picked if she'd been given a choice. I had this dream that Sophie got one of her extensions tangled in the balloon strings today and vanished into the clouds like the house in *Up* and there's a wicked corner of my soul that wishes it was true.

With a loud sigh, I squint around, looking for Helen. There's a boy standing at the edge of the crowd round the hook-a-duck stall, watching me. He was there earlier too – I stared him out and he disappeared but now he's back and something about him makes the hairs on the back of my neck stand up. He must know I've spotted him but this time he doesn't look away. Instead, he walks towards me.

I frown as he comes nearer. He's got untidy brown hair that's either purposefully messy or in need of a good cut. He needs a shave too. I almost like his jacket until I see the Abercrombie and Fitch logo. He looks faintly familiar. Where do I know him from – school? Maybe. He looks around my age although he's shorter than most of the boys in my year. Or he might be one of Leo's seemingly endless acquaintances, coming to reminisce about the good times they had together. When he reaches the stand, his gaze drops to the cakes and he clears his throat like he's nervous. "What's good?"

"Nothing," I snap irritably. "It all tastes of insincerity."

He looks up and I see his eyes are grey, like the sky. His mouth twists in amusement. "That's some sales pitch."

I don't smile back. "Why were you watching me?"

His face falls and his gaze slides away. "I wasn't."

"You were," I insist. "You were there earlier too, I saw you. Who are you, a friend of Leo's or something?"

His eyes fix on mine then, and there's something strange about his expression. "Not exactly." He clears his throat again and hesitates, as though he's trying to decide something. "I'll have one of those chocolate-chip muffins, please."

I bag one up. "Seventy pence."

He hands me a pound. "Keep the change," he says, and walks away.

Helen reappears thirty seconds later with two cans of Coke. She passes one to me and I take it, even though I didn't want a drink. "Did I miss anything?"

"Just some idiot who thinks it's funny to freak people out," I say as I peer into the crowd. "Whoever he is, he's gone now."

She doesn't reply. I look round to see she's biting into another slice of rocky road. "Helen!"

"No one else is eating it," she mumbles defensively, the words indistinct among all the chocolate and marshmallow she's shoved in her mouth.

Luckily for her, I have my mind on other things.

20

JONNY

I blew it.

All I needed to say was, "Hi, I'm Jonny Webb, the guy who messaged you on Facebook. And you're Niamh, Leo Brody's sister."

Although I'm also the guy she blocked on Facebook. So maybe I did myself a favour by walking away. I *did* manage to score a surprisingly good chocolate-chip muffin that I know I shouldn't be eating but it seems rude just to bin it.

There's a pretty respectable turnout at this fundraiser thing; I'm quite impressed. Either Leo had a lot of friends or whoever is organizing this is a PR legend. Maybe both. He certainly has plenty of Facebook friends but I don't know what that actually means. Marco has over 700 and he doesn't strike me as the type to care how many friends he has.

Niamh is prettier in person. You need to look past the death stare and the snarl, of course, but underneath that sullen outer crust there's a fit girl. You can tell she's Leo's sister – the same golden blonde hair, although hers is darker and scraped back in a ponytail, the same smile as the one on all the posters, when she's messing about with her mate and seems to forget how much she hates the world. The paper said Leo was fifteen when he died so at a guess I'd say she's maybe a year younger. With an attitude that's harder than Thor's hammer.

I can still see her through the crowd. She's drinking now and stropping at the other girl, who is stuffing her face with cake. I watch for another minute, then feel my shoulders slump in defeat. There's nothing more to be done here. I had my chance and I bottled it. It's time I went home.

Hands stuffed in my jacket pockets, I head towards the exit. I don't know what I hoped to achieve anyway. I mean, I still don't know for sure that the heart I have used to be Leo's. What was I going to say? "By the way, did you put your newly dead brother's organs up for donation?"

What kind of monster would ask someone that?

On the way out, I pass a stall selling friendship bracelets. They remind me of Em, still in hospital but getting better every day, if her super-chirpy messages are anything to go by. She's into stuff like that, has them daisy-chained around the top of her bed. Soon she'll be at home, without the drips to stop her from wearing them on her wrists. I stop and pick one out in rainbow colours, with a delicate silver heart dangling from the middle.

The girl behind the stall smiles at me. "Three for five pounds and I'll throw in a free wristband if you like?"

She's holding out one of those rubber bracelet things, in pale blue. I can see the words *Living for Leo* cut into it and shake my head. It couldn't be any more ironic if it tried.

"It's for a great cause," she goes on encouragingly and I realize there's no way I can refuse. *What the hell*, I think. It's probably the least I can do after what Leo potentially did for me.

Dipping my head, I start to pick out another two bracelets for Em.

NIAMH

The boy's face is still bugging me. Helen is talking, something about Mr Mushtaq and the bouncy castle, but I'm not listening. I know that boy from somewhere. Where have I seen him before?

Mentally, I flick through Leo's mates. Not one of the football crowd, not one of the musos and I don't think he's from our school. Then a memory stirs, of me and Helen on Hampstead Heath.

"Helen, shut up a second and get your phone out," I demand.

She rolls her eyes but stops talking and does as I ask. "Yes, Your Majesty."

"Open up Facebook," I say, feeling my palms start to

sweat. "Search for Jonny Webb."

Her eyes widen. "The one who was asking about Leo?"

I nod, staring at her phone as she searches. "Yeah. I just want to check something out."

Seven Jonny Webbs pop up on Helen's screen but I only need to see one. Anger surges through me as I recognize his face. "Stay here," I say, tugging off my apron and throwing it onto the table. "I'll be right back."

"Niamh, where are you going?" she calls after me. I ignore her. I'm going to find this creep and tell him where to shove his chocolate-chip muffin.

I spot him over by the exit, bending over one of the stands in that stupid preppy jacket. He's paying Melissa O'Donnell for something; she's smiling at him like he's one of us, someone who knew my brother. And now he's walking away. I break into a run.

He looks surprised to see me at first, and a bit embarrassed, then something else flashes over his face. It's gone before I can work out what it is. "Hi," he says.

"You're the one who messaged me, aren't you? About Leo."

Warily, he nods. "Yes. I'm Jonny Webb."

He holds out his hand and I see there's a *Living for Leo* band encircling his wrist. Another wave of fury washes over me. "So?" I snap. "What are you doing here? Come to ask more questions for *school*?"

The last word rings with as much venom as I can muster. Out of the corner of my eye, I can see Melissa watching us with a frown. Jonny's hand drops to his side. "Look, Niamh, it's not what you think—"

My sudden intake of breath makes a sharp hissing sound. "Right. So you're not some kind of morbid ghoul who preys on the recently bereaved, then?"

His cheeks turn red and he looks uncomfortable. "No, I—"

"Because it seems like it to me," I go on. "It seems a lot like you're a stalkerish creep."

People are stopping what they're doing to gawk now, which makes me even more furious and Jonny blush harder. "Can we go somewhere else to talk about this?" he pleads. "I promise it really isn't what you think."

I fold my arms. "What is it, then? What possible justification could you have for intruding into my life with stupid, pointless questions? Why are you gatecrashing a fundraiser in memory of a boy you didn't even know?"

He stares down at his feet for so long I almost turn and walk away. Then he lifts his head and I'm shocked to see his face is deathly white. When he speaks, it's so quiet I have to lean closer to hear.

"I'm sorry. I've got to go."

* * *

122

"Well?" Helen calls, hurrying up to where I stand, glaring at Jonny's retreating back. "Was it him?"

"Of course it was," I say grimly. "But he made some feeble excuse, said I'd got it wrong."

Melissa O'Donnell comes over. "Bloody hell, Niamh, what did you say to him? He looked like he was going to throw up."

"Do you know him?" I ask, trying not to sound as accusing as I feel.

She shakes her head. "No. But he paid twenty quid for three bracelets when I only asked for a fiver. He seemed nice."

Helen and I exchange glances; Melissa can be a bit thick.

"At least he's gone now," Helen says. "No harm done."

Back at the cake stall, she eyes me curiously. "It's a bit of a trek from St Albans to here. What do you think he wanted?"

I huff irritably. "How should I know? And it's only a few stops on the train, hardly an epic journey."

"Would you go to St Albans for a fundraiser in memory of someone you'd never met?"

"No," I sigh. "But I'm not a nutjob."

She looks thoughtful. "I think we should message him, ask him what he wanted."

I feel like slapping her then, the way they do in films when someone is babbling incomprehensibly. "No, we shouldn't. With a bit of luck, I scared him off and we've seen the last of him."

But I remember the expression on his face when I caught up with him, surprised and embarrassed but something else too. And deep inside I suspect I haven't seen the last of Jonny Webb.

22

JONNY

go to the only person I think will understand: Em.

I don't remember much of how I get to the hospital.
I know I take the Underground, because I see it later on
the journey history of my Oyster card. And I know I walk
for a long time before I'm calm enough to go in and see Em
because I pass the same homeless guy three times on my
way around the block and he asks me for change every
single time. Which means I don't have any cash left to buy
a bottle of water from the hospital shop and have to
scrounge one of Em's Diet Cokes when I reach the ward.

Her smile of welcome vanishes as she watches me gulp
down the warm liquid. "What's wrong?"

I sit down heavily in the chair beside her bed, rubbing

the dried sweat from my face. I don't want to tell her. She's going to go nuts. But I have to tell someone or *I'm* going to go nuts. So I start at the beginning and tell her about Niamh.

When I'm done, she looks at me for a long time. "Did they check you for brain damage when they swapped over your heart?" she asks finally.

"I suppose so," I mumble in reply.

"Then you have no excuse. You're just an idiot," she says, shaking her head as though she can't quite believe what she's heard. "Seriously, Jonny, what were you thinking? You don't even know if Leo is your donor."

That's the problem – I can't explain it properly. I don't know why I need to know who my donor was – life would be so much simpler if I could just be grateful and move on – but it's like there's a part of me that doesn't belong and I won't be able to move on until I know where the heart came from. And deep down, I've got this feeling that it was Leo. Like my heart recognizes him. None of that will make sense to Em, who's had to fight and battle every step of the way for her miracle, whereas I got mine without lifting a finger.

"What's she like, this Niamh girl?"

The question catches me by surprise. I glance across at Em but her face isn't giving anything away. What does she want to know about Niamh for? Leo's the interesting one.

"I dunno," I say, frowning. "She's a bit younger than us, looks like Leo. Pretty but has a chip on her shoulder that's even bigger than yours. Why?"

She studies me closely for a second, then settles back against her pillow. "Just curious. What are you going to do next?"

I shrug. "Not much I can do. Keep looking for other possible donors in case I'm wrong, although it's hard to get details." I let out a growl of frustration. "That's why the Facebook page was such a gift. It's like the universe wants me to find out about Leo."

Em stares at me. "Easy there, Psychic Sally. The universe has nothing to do with this, it's about you, wanting something you're not supposed to have. You're not meant to go all Sherlock and track down the family of your donor." She sighs, looking suddenly exhausted. "What if they don't want to be found?"

I only need to know whose heart I have, not arrange a reunion. I think about trying to argue my side, but I feel bad then, because I've forgotten she's still recovering. The last thing she needs is me dumping a load of crap on her. "You're right," I say, dredging up a smile. "Smart-arse."

She smiles back but it's a tired effort. "You'd better believe it."

The sight of the friendship bracelets on the bed above her head reminds me of the ones I bought earlier. Reaching into my pocket, I hand her the crumpled paper bag. "Here. I brought you something."

She opens it and her face lights up. She pulls out the one with the tiny silver heart, touches it gently with one finger. "You shouldn't have. Thanks."

"Want me to put them with the others?" I ask, reaching for them but her hand tightens possessively around the colourful threads.

"No, I want to look at them first," she says. "One of the nurses can do it later."

She stares down at them and I notice her eyelids are starting to droop. On impulse, I lean forward and drop a gentle kiss onto her fuzzy head. "Okay, Chemo-Girl. See you soon."

Her eyes fly open. "What was that for?"

I laugh uncomfortably. We've never done physical contact before; maybe I've overstepped the mark. "No reason."

She watches me for a long moment before she nods. "Okay."

I'm almost through the curtains when she calls me back. "Jonny," she says, a guarded, unreadable expression on her face. "If you knew for certain that it was Leo, would it make you happy?"

My nod is instant. "Yeah, I think it would."

Her eyes drift shut. "Okay. See you later."

I think about her question a few times on the way home and each time, I come to the same conclusion – it would make me happy to know that Leo was my donor. More than happy, in fact – almost…whole, like my heart belongs to me. But it raises another question, one I don't have the answer to: how far am I prepared to go to be sure?

23

NIAMH

On Sunday morning, I wake up ridiculously early. I lie there for a minute, listening to my parents clattering around downstairs and try to go back to sleep but it's no good. Sighing, I reach for my phone. When I get to Facebook, I stare at the message in my inbox for a long time.

15 October 22:34
Hi Niamh
You don't know me but I'm a friend of Jonny Webb.
I know you're pretty angry with him, and you have
every right to be, but he's not the person you think
he is.

He has a really good reason for contacting you.
He doesn't know I'm doing this but he deserves
a chance to explain. Please.
Thanks,
Emily Mitchell

At first, I don't know what to make of it. Is this what stalkers do, get their mates to contact their victims to reassure them they're trustworthy and not really raging psychopaths? I even wonder if Emily Mitchell actually exists but a quick look at her profile convinces me she does. There are a lot of "get well soon" messages on there, plus a couple of photos that look like they were taken in hospital and I'm pretty sure Jonny can't be messed up enough to invent a friend who is ill in order to get my sympathy. Then I start thinking about the way he looked when I confronted him, the pale, miserable look on his face before he walked off. He had something on his mind, a purpose for being there and I'd be lying if I said I wasn't a little bit curious about what it was. Maybe this Emily girl is right. Maybe Jonny does deserve a chance to explain.

Wondering if I'm doing the right thing, I remove the block and type Jonny a message.

You've got one chance. Don't screw it up.

And I go downstairs in search of sugar.

'm lying on my bed, thinking of breakfast, when the message comes through. I didn't sleep much last night, kept replaying what happened at the fundraiser in my head, like it was my own personal movie. I ought to get up – do something – when I can't sleep. While I was in hospital, I used to fantasize about all the things I'd do when I was well but today I can't seem to find the enthusiasm. I should make the effort, get out there and grab life by the balls instead of lying here feeling sorry for myself. Mum will be in soon with my medication and a cup of tea – maybe I'll suggest we do something together.

The message wipes that idea clean out of my head. For Niamh to have messaged me, she'd have to have unblocked me. And she's giving me a chance to explain – why? Unless she felt bad about the way she spoke to me yesterday but she doesn't exactly sound sorry. So why the sudden change?

I'm not complaining, though, and start tapping out a reply straight away. I'm so engrossed in what I'm doing that I barely notice Mum come in. It's not until she clears her throat and sings, "Medicine time!" that I look up.

"Just leave it there," I say, nodding at the bedside table.

She shakes the pillbox. "No time like the present."

I bite back a sigh. She means well but downing a cocktail of drugs is the last thing on my mind right now. "In a minute."

"Now, sweetheart," she goes on, "I know you don't like it but you know you have to take—"

"For God's sake!" I snap. "Stop talking to me like I'm two! I know about the drugs, Mum. I know."

I regret the words as soon as they're out of my mouth but there's no way to take them back. It doesn't matter that mood swings are part of the deal with the drugs I'm on and it doesn't matter that she's used to my crankiness; her expression shifts as she turns away and I can't bear it. "Look, Mum, I'm sorry," I say desperately. "Just give me a minute to finish this message, yeah?"

"Okay, Jonny," she says, without turning round, and I can tell from the wobble in her voice that it's not okay. "Let me know if you need anything."

I stare at my phone for a minute, feeling like a tool. Then I push Mum out of my head – right now, I need to concentrate. This is my one and only chance to find out more about Leo. I can't afford to cock it up.

25

NIAMH

16 October 10:17

Hi Niamh

I don't know why you've unblocked me and got back
in touch but first of all, I promise you I'm not a stalker.
I know it looks bad. I know you think I'm a nutter.
But I don't have your photograph lining my bedroom
walls or your address programed into Maps on my
phone. And I'm really not a "morbid ghoul who preys
on the recently bereaved", like you called me
yesterday. Seriously, I own a teddy bear called Percy
who I've had since I was two years old and who I can't
go to sleep without. How many psychopaths can
say that?

Oh my God, he's sent me a picture of his teddy bear. His actual teddy bear, complete with a tartan bow tie, mildly chewed nose and a squinty eye. I don't know whether to laugh or throw up.

> You wanted to know why I was at the fundraiser
> yesterday, why I bothered you in the first place and
> I fully intend to tell you. The trouble is I can't do it
> online. So how about we chat on here, get to know
> each other a bit first. Then, when you're happy I'm not
> a weirdo, we can meet up somewhere public and I'll
> give you your answers. Fair?
> Jonny

And that's it. If he'd signed off with a kiss, I would have deleted the message and blocked him in a heartbeat. But one way or the other, he's got my attention. There's only one thing for it, I decide, picking up my phone to text Helen. We need an emergency consultation.

Helen meets me at the park. It's colder than yesterday and I was so determined to ignore my mother's constant bleating to wrap up warm that I've come out without my coat. Helen, of course, is sensibly dressed in about fifty layers, while I sit shivering on a swing. The sky looks heavy and full of rain. We're the only ones mad enough to be here.

"Mysterious," Helen comments when she reads Jonny's message. "And quite clever really, because now you're intrigued."

"I am not," I snort. "I'm irritated."

She eyes me sideways. "And interested. Admit it."

Ignoring her, I read the message again. "Okay, maybe a little bit interested. But still mostly freaked out. Who's this Emily girl, do you think?"

Helen shrugs. "Probably just a mate. Or an unwitting pawn in his fiendish plan. It's hard to tell."

My eyes narrow. "I get the feeling you're not taking this very seriously. What could he possibly have to tell me that he needs to say in person?"

"That he's an axe murderer?" Helen jokes. I don't laugh. "Sorry. But I don't know the answer to any of these questions and there's only really one way to find out the truth."

"And what's that?" I say, blowing on my fingers to defrost them a bit.

"Get typing."

My mother is predictably fussy when I go back home.

"What did I tell you about wrapping up warm?" she tuts, hurrying over to grasp my hands. "You're freezing."

I hate it when she goes into crazy overprotective mode like this, as though she's suddenly remembered it's only Leo who died and needs to convince herself she's looking after me. I pull my fingers from hers in a sudden flare of anger. "Sorry to disappoint you but I think I'll live."

"Niamh!" she says, eyes widening as though I've slapped her. "What a horrible thing to say."

Dad lowers his paper and glares at me with a fury I'm sure he never needed with Leo. "Apologize. Now."

I think about standing my ground, making them see what it's like to see-saw between their broken indifference and suffocating concern. But I want them to leave me alone and the easiest way to achieve that is to play along. "Sorry," I say, doing my best to sound apologetic. "I'm going to my room."

Their eyes burn into my skull as I trudge upstairs.

"I don't know what to do with her, Ed...really I don't," I hear my mother say as I close my bedroom door. Dad's voice rumbles in reply and I drown them both out with some music, throwing myself onto my bed with my eyes closed. After a few minutes, I roll over and pull out my phone. So Jonny Webb wants to chat, does he? Let's see what he's got to say.

JONNY AND NIAMH

26

16 October 12:43

OK, Ghoul-Boy, you've got my attention.

But don't think I'm fooled by the picture of Percy –
there's a big question over how he got that damaged
eye. And I'm not sure about the whole "I'll tell you
when we meet" routine, either – what can be so bad
that you can't just tell me? Unless you really are a
psycho. In which case, this all makes perfect sense.
Luckily for you, I'm a) ridiculously curious and
b) bored out of my brain right now. So I'll play
along. Give me three good reasons to keep the
conversation going.

12:49

Niamh,

You want three reasons to keep talking to me?

OK, here goes:

1. Without wanting to sound like a loser, I'm kind of in between friends right now. So you'd be doing me a real favour.

2. I think underneath your stroppy surface, you're actually a nice person. The kind to take pity on a Billy No Mates like me.

3. I am also bored out of my brain right now. See 1.

Percy is actually an agent of S.H.I.E.L.D. and he got his injury in the line of duty. I can't say any more than that without having to erase all memory of having met me from your mind. Again, see 1.

12:58

1. Friends are overrated. I only have one.

2. Wrong. Underneath my stroppy surface there's an even stroppier person. Don't try to appeal to my better nature – I don't have one.

3. I *may* be slightly less bored now. Don't go thinking it means anything.

Also, no wonder you have no friends if you tell them your teddy bear is an agent of S.H.I.E.L.D.

13:06

I've only got one friend too but I like to
think it's quality, not quantity that matters
with mates. See? We have something in
common already…

17 October 16:12
Hey Ghoul-Boy. What's happening?

16:13

Not much. Trying to persuade my parents to let me
go to London Super Comic Con. You?

16:14
Ugh, parents. And London Super Comic Con
sounds like you. Are you going with Percy?

16:15

Maybe, unless I get a better offer.

16:18
Don't look at me. I've seen the Wolverine
movie but only because Leo and my dad
made us watch it. It's hard to swallow all that
invincibility rubbish these days.

16:25

Sorry. I didn't mean to make you feel bad ☹
I don't believe in invincibility either. I just like
the characters.

> **16:27**
>
> You don't make me feel bad. You're only the
> second person to make me smile all day.

16:28

Then my work here is done ☺

> **18 October 10:16**
>
> You busy, Ghoul-Boy?

10:20

Nah. In maths, trying to calculate the value of n but
it's not exactly a Michael Bay explosion-fest.
What's up?

> **10:20**
>
> Nothing. Just got a few minutes to kill
> before I see my counsellor. I thought you
> could amuse me.

10:22

At your service, Miss Brody. I hate those few
minutes before you go into an appointment –
I always feel on edge too.

> **10:24**
>
> Yeah. Such a waste of time. It's not like she's
> got a magic wand to bring my brother back
> so what's the point?

10:26

Sounds like you miss him.

> **11:23**
>
> So that's fifty minutes of my life I'll never
> get back.

11:25

Ha – that good?

> **11:28**
>
> The usual – blah blah, don't blame yourself,
> blah blah, talk about how you feel. Nothing
> that might actually help.

11:29

Oh yeah, tell me about it. I see a counsellor too
sometimes – he says the same kind of stuff.
Such bull.

11:30

I don't think I knew that – we should swap
counsellor stories. I hate seeing mine – in
case you hadn't noticed, I don't exactly like
to open up.

11:30

Yeah, I kind of got that ☺
The lads at college say hi, btw.

11:31

YOU'RE LETTING THEM READ THIS?

11:32

Relax, I don't have a death wish.
No, they wanted to know who I was messaging
so I said it was a friend and they said hello.
Don't worry, they don't know you're a girl. They'd
steal my phone to get your number if I let that slip.

11:34

Oh…that's nice. They sound like real charmers.

Wait…I thought you were in between friends?

I hope you haven't told them about Percy.

11:37

I haven't. See? You've upped my social intelligence already.

11:38

Don't get excited – you've still got a long way to go, Ghoul-Boy.

Gotta go, I'm at school.

11:40

OK, laters. Hey, in case you were wondering, the value of n was four.

11:51

I guess maybe you weren't wondering about the value of n…

This is the kind of thing you mean, isn't it?

19 October 03:31

Jonny – are you there?

03:33

Just about. What's wrong?

03:34

Bad dream. Feel sick.

03:36

Oh ☹

Anything I can do?

03:37

Not really. Just distract me.

03:38

I think I can do better than that. Hold on…

03:41

I can't BELIEVE you just sent me a photo
of Percy ☺

03:43

He's virtual medicine – as badass as kryptonite
where bad dreams are concerned.

03:44

You're such a geek.

03:46

I know. But it's all part of my charm, right?
Right?

27

JONNY

Em's been a bit quiet on the message front lately – so much so that I half expect her to be getting her groove back at home next time I pop in after my review. But instead, she's in a room on her own and looks like she's lost some weight. She waves a hand when I ask her about it and mumbles something about an infection, which also explains why I had to scrub up before the nurses would let me in to see her. A lowered immune system is one of the things Em and I have both struggled with.

"So," she says, once she's finished convincing me she's all right. "What's new? Apart from the weight you've put on, I mean."

"I've got the steroids to thank for that," I say, then

148

hesitate, wondering what else to tell her. I can't mention Niamh, not after everything Em said last time. The problem now is Niamh's become a pretty big part of my life lately. I've even made her a playlist on Spotify – one of these days I'll find enough courage to share it with her.

I don't know whether it's because we only talk online but I've found myself telling her the sort of stuff I'd usually only share with Em. So Niamh knows how much my parents' well-meaning interference bugs me and in return, she's opened up a bit about her own life. We don't talk about Leo much but I think she likes our conversations, maybe not as much as me but enough not to question why I got in touch in the first place. Not yet, anyway. And I can't talk to Em about any of this because I don't want her to flip out.

So that leaves me with college as my conversation starter, where the actual studying is going okay. The homework sucks, of course, but I don't actually mind it – it feels like a normal thing to hate.

The social side could be better. News has got around about my heart condition, although Marco swears it didn't come from him, so I'm getting a lot of funny looks and some pretty personal questions. In some ways I wish I'd been honest and told the truth about the transplant but until I know for sure who my donor was, it doesn't feel like I own this heart. It's like getting an anonymous gift –

you *always* wonder where it came from – and I'm definitely not ready to talk about it with people I hardly know.

In spite of his big mouth, Marco is turning into the closest thing I have to a mate there. I chat with the other kids in my classes, of course, and some of them are all right but at the end of the lesson we go our separate ways. No one invites me to do stuff outside college or at the weekends; I don't think it crosses their minds. At least Marco lets me hang out at smokers' corner occasionally, even if I do feel like the rabbit in a den of jackals. Sometimes there are just six of us – Jackson, Eavis, Billy, Charlie and Marco – other times it's a bigger group. Marco is definitely the top dog, no matter who else is there. And actually, some of them are a bit of a laugh; I get on well with Marco and Charlie, although we don't exactly have much in common. Still, it's good to have some company, especially now I'm sure their frequent drug references are pretty much rubbish.

"What's new?" I repeat, meeting Em's gaze. "Not much. It's harder than I thought, being out there. Sometimes I miss it here." There's a jagged nail on my thumb. I stare down at it and pick at the edge, thinking of all the times we dreamed about having our freedom, going home. "I miss being around people who understand and I miss knowing there's always someone to talk to who just gets it. I – I miss you, Em."

The last sentence comes out in a rush and I can feel my face going red the moment I stop speaking. Em doesn't answer straight away. She must hate me, sitting here moaning about how hard it is to be healthy.

"I miss you too," she says after a while. "But I don't seem to be going anywhere – you know where I am when you want to talk. And you've got your counsellor, right?"

I shift uncomfortably, not wanting to tell her that I skipped my last counselling session so I didn't have to lie about looking for my donor. I don't know why it felt like such a big deal – I seem to be lying a lot lately. But it's one thing talking to Em about contacting Leo's sister. It's something else entirely to tell someone in the medical profession about it. Then things get real and questions get asked and serious people might start taking an interest. People who might make me stop. I don't want that.

I look up at Em and force myself to smile. "Yeah. I'm just talking crap, as usual."

She watches me carefully. "Did you get in touch with Niamh again?"

"Nah," I say, trying to sound casual and disinterested at the same time. "I reckon you were right about that."

She opens her mouth then closes it, like there's something she wants to say and decides not to. The silence stretches and I look around, searching for something – anything – to talk about. This never used to happen with us – we always had good banter. Something's changed, something more than the fact that I'm better and Em isn't, but I don't know what it is. Then I notice the picture I drew of Chemo-Girl is missing.

"Oh, they must have forgotten to put it back up when they moved me in here," Em says when I ask her about it. "It's probably in the cupboard."

"You can't get the staff these days, can you?" I say, standing up with a loud tut. "I'll find it."

"No!" Her voice is sharp and loud. "Don't bother with it now. One of the nurses can do it later."

Sinking back into the chair, I know I'm frowning. Is it the picture she has a problem with or me?

Em sighs. "Sorry, Jonny, I'm tired. Maybe you should go now."

To be fair, she does look tired. There are shadows underneath her eyes and her skin is sallow. I remember a few infections of my own – they can really knock you out and the last thing you want is to make small talk with visitors. "Sure," I reply, and a wave of understanding passes between us. "My parents will be finished in the cafe now anyway. You take it easy, Chemo-Girl."

She nods and pretends to zap me with a laser gun. "Kapow."

As I walk down the corridor towards the cafe, I check my phone and see a message from Niamh.

21 October 15:17
Hey, Ghoul-Boy. Guess who scored a free Snickers
from the school vending machine today?

Grinning, I type a reply.

> **15:26**
> I hope you reported it to the school
> office before you ate it? Because it's theft
> if you didn't.

Her response takes less than ten seconds.

15:26
Finders keepers. It's like the universe wanted to
cheer me up.

My fingers fly across the screen as I tap in an answering
message.

> **15:27**
> Hey, I thought that was my job.

And Em slips clean from my mind.

25 October 17:33
Hey Niamh
How was your day?

> **17:40**
> It sucked – school was bad and my mother is
> still clinically insane. But at least she's not
> crying and my day is getting better now.

17:46
Better because it's almost over? Or better because
you're talking to me? (Please say the second one
– I'm needy, remember?)

17:51

Duh. Better because I have a tub of
Ben & Jerry's and no one to share it with.
It's not all about you, Ghoul-Boy.
OK, it's a little bit about you ☺

18:02

☺

Cookie Dough? Phish Food? Please don't tell me
it's Chunky Monkey.

18:02

Baked Alaska. Obviously.
Cookie Dough was Leo's favourite – I don't
eat it any more.

18:03

☹

Percy says have a hug.

18:03

Thanks, Ghoul-Boy. Thanks, Percy.

18:05

He says you're welcome. Do you think you could
maybe start calling me Jonny? Having a nickname

is cute but Ghoul-Boy isn't
doing much for my ego.

18:07
Yeah, I suppose I could.
So, Jonny, how was your day? How are the
jailers treating you?

18:08
Not so bad. I wish they would accept that I'm not
a little kid any more and let me make my own
choices but apart from that...
Wait...you did mean my parents, right? Because
my mate Marco is more likely to be an inmate,
not a jailer.

18:10
Wow, he sounds awesome – can you get me
his number?

18:11
For real??

18:13
No, not for real.
But yes, I did mean your parents. Mine went

the extra mile to ensure my life is devoid of any freedom or pleasure today (another ridiculous family healthy eating plan of my mother's that will last a week), so pretty much the same as usual. I sometimes wonder if they were born old – I can't believe they were ever our age. And before you point it out, I know they've had it rough. My mum never lets me forget it.

18:23

Ha ha, I bet my parents are even older than yours – there's no hope for them. And I know exactly what you mean about not being allowed to forget what happened last week, last month, last year. I think it's biologically programed into them to fuss.
Anyway, it sounds like you need cheering up so here's a joke. What did the cheese say to its reflection?

18:24

Seriously? You want me to answer?

18:25

Uh, yeah – that's usually how comedy works.
Remind me never to try a knock-knock joke with you.

18:29
Jeez. OK, Laughter Police.
Cheese?

18:31
Cheese? The cheese says "Cheese"? Are you
even familiar with the concept of comedy?

18:38
Fine, I give in. What did the stupid cheese
say to its stupid reflection?

18:38
Halloumi.
Geddit?

18:39
I get it. You're not pinning your future career
on this, are you?

18:57
Trust me, I'm funnier in person. Want me to
prove it?

29

NIAMH

So here's a thing I never thought would happen – I like someone who is not Helen. And even more unpredictably, it's Jonny. He's a bit soft sometimes, like with those cringe-worthy photos of his teddy he sends, but mostly he's all right. Sometimes we ping-pong messages all night and if he is an axe murderer, he's an axe murderer who makes me smile. Although thinking about it, he could be a high-functioning sociopath and I wouldn't know until it was too late. I'm prepared to take that chance.

The best bit is talking to someone who didn't know me before the accident. Admittedly, we moan about our parents a lot but that's just a surface thing. Underneath, it feels like we're saying more. He makes me laugh too, in a good way, like I can be a better version of me, the person I might have been if – not if Leo had never been born, because that's the kind of thought I steer clear of now he's gone, but maybe who I would have been if Leo hadn't been such a golden balls. To tell the honest truth, sometimes I even forget Leo is dead. Just for a minute or two.

I haven't told Helen I've given Jonny my mobile number, or that we've agreed to meet up tomorrow. She still thinks there's a chance he might be a weirdo, although she concedes he's probably not a catfish. I still haven't asked him about the mysterious Emily – I thought I'd wait and see if he mentioned her but he never does. I don't think she can be his girlfriend, unless he really is sociopathic.

Mum is still doing her split-personality thing – one minute it's all fundraising, the next it's interrogation central – *Where are you going? What time will you be back? Is your phone switched on?* And crying…still crying when she thinks no one can hear. Imagine if she knew what I was doing – arranging to meet up with someone I'd got to know online. She'd flip out, lose the plot, ground me for ever. It's not that I don't understand why she's like this – I do. But when she asks me if I want to talk, I know she means about Leo and I can't bear the reminder of how amazing they thought he was, with the added implication that I need to up my game – be everything he was – when the truth is I'm a poor second best. At least Dad doesn't pretend to care – he's not here much and when he is, he hardly speaks. Mum could learn a thing or two from him, to be honest; even a conversation about putting my washing into the machine ends up being about Leo. I know it hurts that he's gone. I know it's an ache that will never go away. But I don't know what I can do to help.

"It's understandable you feel that way," Teresa says, on the rare occasion I actually talk about what's on my mind. "But you shouldn't feel it is your responsibility to carry your parents' loss as well as your own, Niamh. Have you told them how you feel?"

She makes it sound so easy, like it's a conversation we can have while we watch TV. The trouble is, I don't know where to start, don't know how to make it more about me instead of Leo. That's why I like talking to Jonny – it's not *The Leo Brody Show*. Although I haven't forgotten why Jonny contacted me in the first place. And I've tried to work out what he's going to say but seriously, it's like he's lived in a void most of his life. There's hardly anything on Facebook, and I suppose that's just about possible, if you grew up on Mars or somewhere the internet hasn't reached yet, but I can't help wondering what he's hiding. Maybe that's part of the appeal, the fact that he's got secrets. Or maybe he's just different from anyone else I know. In a good way.

Whatever the reason, I'm looking forward to meeting him. At least, I think I am.

30
JONNY

My palms are sweating as I wait for Niamh. We've arranged to meet in this trendy little coffee house on Hampstead High Street – neutral territory, I suppose, in case I turn out to be crazy – and I was so worried about being late that I got here ridiculously early. So now I'm on my second decaf skinny latte and bursting for a pee. But I can't go, in case she arrives while I'm in the toilet and thinks I've stood her up. Mind you, at this rate, I'll wet myself before she even gets here. Great.

The barista remembered my name when I went up for my second coffee. I couldn't work out where she's from but I like the way her accent wrapped itself around my name and turned it into something exotic. *Jah-nee*.

I might make it my coffee-house name.

According to her name badge, she's called Gabriela. *Gabree-ella*. It's a good name, familiar and striking at the same time. I'm watching her now as she cleans the machine; she's facing away so she can't see me staring. Her hair is long and dark, the same colour Em's used to be before her chemo kicked in, but Barista-Girl's is straight and shiny. Briefly, I wonder how it would feel to run my fingers through it, let the strands slip over my skin like silk. Em's curls were so wild that they looked like they'd bite if you touched them. Kind of like her actually, but I'm not sure she's always been a fighter. It's just what cancer made her.

The door opens. I glance up to see Niamh stood there, frowning uncertainly as though she's not sure she's in the right place. She looks good – pretty, although I suspect she's made zero effort. The coat she's wearing is about two sizes too big, it makes her seem younger, and her boots are thick and ugly. The sun is gleaming off her hair, giving her a sort of halo, but underneath it her face is pale. Should I wave or will it just make her think I'm a prick? There's only me and a woman with a baby in the whole place. Then Niamh's eyes come to rest on me and she hesitates. I know she's debating whether she should go through with this and I need her to stay. So I lift my arm and wave, madly, making sure she can't pretend not to see me. She doesn't wave back.

My mouth goes dry as she walks over to my table. I'm not sure how to do this – should I start with Leo or make small talk first? No, I correct myself silently when she pulls out the chair opposite me and sits down. What you need to do first is say hello.

I hand her a menu and try my best to smile. "Hi. I wasn't sure you'd show."

She shrugs. "Of course I showed. How come you're not at school?"

"It's a college, not a school. I only have to go four days a week. It's a perk of being –" I manage to stop myself from saying "sick" – "special. How come *you're* not at school?"

"Supposed to be seeing my counsellor," she says and one eyebrow lifts in accusation. "You sound like my mum."

I clear my throat awkwardly. After all the friendly and funny banter we've swapped online, I'd forgotten how prickly she is in person. I actually want her to call me Ghoul-Boy, that's how bad it is. "Do you want a drink?"

"Hot chocolate with whipped cream and a chocolate flake," she says without a second's hesitation. I can't blame her – it's what I'd have if I could. Raising a hand, I smile at Gabriela.

She heads straight over, pen and pad in hand and a smile on her face. "Yes, Jah-nee, what can I get you?"

I can feel Niamh's stare as Gabriela walks away with her order – what now? But I can't worry about second-

164

guessing what she's thinking because a more pressing need is trying to get my attention. "Excuse me for a minute. Just need to – uh…"

My voice trails off as I feel my cheeks start to flame. Why am I suddenly so embarrassed about going for a wazz? Bodily functions have no mystery among hospital kids, although Em and I made a pact never to talk about taking a dump. "Back in a minute," I mumble and flee.

I suck in long deep breaths while I pee and run over what I'm going to say. I'll build up to it, I decide, give her a bit of background and then break out the truth. Yeah, that's how I'll do it. I catch sight of myself in the mirror as I'm washing my hands; my hair is stuck to my forehead and my cheeks are so red I look like a sweaty tomato. *Not a good look.* But I don't want to keep Niamh waiting so I splash some cold water over my burning face and think of icebergs.

When I get back to the table, Niamh is digging her spoon into a mountain of cream and chocolate that makes my mouth water. "Looks good," I say, sitting down.

"It is," she grudgingly admits. Then, "You do know that waitress is only flirting with you so you'll tip her, by the way."

My mouth drops open a bit. Flirting? She calls a couple of smiles *flirting*? I call it being friendly. And why does she feel the need to point it out – in case I get too up myself?

"Thanks," I manage drily. "Are you always so rude?"

Is it my imagination or does she almost smile? "Now you really do sound like my mum."

"Sorry," I say. "But that was pretty blunt. Luckily, I don't really mind – my friend, Em, is the same."

A flicker of something crosses her face. "You've never mentioned her. Is she your girlfriend?"

"No!" I exclaim, and wonder how to explain. It's too early to bring up the hospital stuff – I want to build up to that, not blurt it out within fifteen minutes of meeting her. "She's just a mate, someone who gets where I'm coming from."

Niamh takes a long sip of her drink. "Sounds like girlfriend material to me."

I stare at her. What *is* going on? I thought we'd got past all this passive-aggressive crap, although to be honest, there's not much that's passive about Niamh's attitude right now. She's acting like I've threatened to bite the head off her hamster and I really don't understand why. I need to get her back onside – preferably before my sweat glands wash us all out of the door. Wiping my palms surreptitiously on my jeans, I take a deep breath. "Why don't we start again?"

She studies me for a long uncomfortable moment. "Or you could just tell me why you got in touch. What's your fascination with my twin?"

The world implodes. Leo was her *twin*? Why didn't I know that? Then again, how could I, unless I'd thought to compare their birthdays on Facebook, which never even crossed my mind. My eyes fix on the weird necklace thing she's wearing, a white stone with a hole in the middle, before I realize it looks like I'm staring at her chest and my gaze skitters away. Sucking in another deep breath, I try to get a grip, running through a rapid relaxation technique my counsellor taught me in case I ever needed it. By the time I've hurried through the name of every Avengers character I can think of, I'm much calmer. "I didn't know you and Leo were twins."

"Why would you?" Niamh frowns. "We spent most of the last seven years trying to pretend we weren't related. But you still haven't answered my question."

Now my upper lip is sweating too and my heart is thudding harder in my chest, which is a sign I'm seriously stressed. Transplanted hearts don't have the same nerve connections as native ones, they react slowly to any stimulus, so if mine is pounding there's a mother lode of adrenalin running through my body.

Niamh is tapping the end of her spoon on the table now. I'm fairly sure she's wishing she'd stayed at home. This is it, the moment I explain who I am, why she's here and what it all has to do with Leo...

I can't do it. I just can't.

31

NIAMH

I've had enough of this. First of all, Jonny sits there eyeing up the waitress like we haven't spent the last few weeks messaging back and forth and he wishes it was her sitting here instead of me, then he goes on and on about this Emily girl without explaining who she is and now it looks like he's totally lost it. I'm starting to think I've made a mistake meeting him at all.

With a regretful glance at what's left of my hot chocolate, I reach for my coat.

"Wait," Jonny says. "Don't go."

Out of the corner of my eye, I can see the waitress watching us. Maybe she's hoping to chat Jonny up some more once I've gone, flirt her way to a bigger tip. Or maybe she fancies him. He's not bad-looking, actually – his hair still needs a cut and his face is weirdly chubby, considering how skinny the rest of his body is. He needs a shave too, although some girls find stubble sexy, and I wonder if he owns anything that doesn't have a pretentious American logo on it. But now that I've had a chance to look at him properly, I notice he's got really nice eyes; grey, with tiny gold flecks in the middle. I can see why the waitress might be interested, even without knowing how sweet he can be. "Start talking," I say.

He puffs out a long breath and throws me an uncomfortable look. "The trouble is, I think you're going to freak out."

The last scraps of my patience start to slip away. "Are you being serious?" I ask, glaring at him. "You sucker me into messaging you, lure me into meeting you and now you don't want to tell me what it's all about? Are you surprised I'm going to freak out?"

There's a silence, during which I notice there are beads of sweat on his forehead. Whatever it is he wants to tell me, it's obviously big. I think back to all the times he's made me laugh lately, when laughs have been pretty hard to come by, and all the times he's understood exactly what I've been trying to say, even when I can't explain myself properly. And something softens inside me. "Or maybe I'll just listen now and save the freaking out for later."

He doesn't smile, sits quietly for a few more seconds, eyes fixed on the sugar bowl as though it's giving him advice. "Okay," he says finally. "You want to know the truth? The reason I sent you the message asking about Leo?"

If he was anyone else I might launch myself across the table and strangle him with my bare hands. But my curiosity is stronger than my irritation and I've already decided to be nice, so I dig deep and make my expression as encouraging as I can. "Yes, Ghoul-Boy, I want to know."

Bland interchangeable pop music fills the silence. Behind us, the coffee machine hisses and spurts. The baby squeals in the corner. My eyes never leave Jonny.

He looks up. "It's simple, really...I fancied you."

At first, I think I've misheard. "What?"

"I fancied you," he repeats, briefly closing his eyes. "A friend of a friend shared the link about the fundraiser and I clicked on the page and saw your picture. I wanted to message you but everything I thought of writing sounded cheesy. So I went for an unusual and, with the benefit of hindsight, a slightly bad-taste approach."

My jaw drops. "Bad taste? Some – no, *most* – people would call it creepy."

"I know," he says, his gaze skating away.

My head spins as I try to piece together what he's saying. It's not beyond the realms of possibility, I suppose, but it *is* weird. In fact, we've entered Bizarreville and gone right out the other side. "So you weren't interested in Leo at all?" I say slowly.

Jonny hesitates. "I wouldn't say that exactly. But from that moment, the first second I saw your photo, I haven't been able to get you out of my mind." He stops talking abruptly and puts his head in his hands with a groan. "Sorry. This isn't what I planned to say at all."

He looks like he's hoping the ground will swallow him up and I can't say I blame him. Who chats someone up by asking about a family tragedy? Even the skankiest boys at school wouldn't go there. Then again, I have to admit to a certain amount of grudging respect for Jonny Webb's technique becausw his plan has kind of worked: we have exchanged 103 messages and 90 texts. I'm here, with him, right now. And if I'm one hundred per cent honest, I'm also a tiny bit flattered. No one's ever fancied me before, or at least they've never admitted it, and they've certainly never put up with my moods for long enough to come up with an elaborate plan to get my attention. Then a considerably less pleasant thought occurs to me: Jonny isn't Leo's stalker at all. He's mine.

Oh God, Helen is going to flip.

* * *

Helen doesn't flip. What she does is much, much worse.

I phone her on the way home and she doesn't speak for so long after I finish talking that I think we've been cut off. "Tell me," she says at last, "tell me you told him where to shove his hot chocolate?"

I almost do tell her that, because the eruption that's rumbling down the handset is almost too big to contemplate. But this is Helen: we don't lie to each other. Much. "No, I didn't. I agreed to see him again."

There's a sharp intake of breath in my ear. "*What? When?*"

"Friday evening," I reply. "Look, Helen, it's not how it seems. I like him, he gets me. He's...nice."

"Stalkers often are. At first."

I sigh. "He's not a stalker – he—"

"He contacts you out of the blue, with a totally bogus question about your recently deceased brother and then turns up somewhere he knows you'll be," Helen cuts in, her voice clipped and precise. "He then starts a conversation to get you to trust him and the moment you let your guard down, he practically asks you to marry him. Believe me, he's a stalker."

She sounds like she's reading off an evidence sheet and the rational part of me thinks she's right. But then there's the part that sat opposite him for forty-five minutes today, listening to him talk and explain what he'd done and why.

The part that noticed the nervousness when he spoke, the gentleness of his voice, the genuine emotion behind his words, the way he said the things I was thinking before I knew I was thinking them. It's also the part that is suggesting he might be just what I need to help me move on – something good in my life, something to get me out of bed each day. And I know it should be enough that I'm alive when my brother is dead but it isn't. I want someone to see *me* when they look my way, instead of Leo's sister.

Helen is talking again but I'm not really listening. I'm thinking about the way Jonny's eyelashes rest darkly against his pale skin when he stares down, and the feeling I can't shake that there's something he's not telling me. I like the idea that I caught his eye, that he was interested enough to track me down, even that he's a tiny bit obsessed with me. I like the sense of mystery, wondering if there's more to him than meets the eye. I like feeling something instead of anger and misery and emptiness. I like him.

"…and that's why you have to tell your parents," Helen finishes.

Her words jolt me out of my mini-daydream. "What?" I yelp. "That's the last thing I should do. I can't even walk to the shops on my own without Mum stressing out. Imagine how she'd react if I told her about Jonny."

"Niamh—"

"No, Helen, listen," I interrupt, before she starts

quoting stranger-danger statistics at me. "You know how crappy things have been for me lately – even before the accident. I haven't been in a good place for a long time. And now I feel like something might finally be changing. All right, I agree that Jonny's chat-up skills could use some work but I like getting his messages, they make me smile. I want to give him a chance."

"And if he isn't the person you think he is?" she says. "What then?"

I take a deep breath. "Then I'll probably turn up dead in a ditch somewhere and you can shout *I told you so* at my funeral." I hesitate, trying to think of something to get her onside. "Can't I have this, Helen? Can't I enjoy the fact that someone is interested in me for a change?"

Silence crackles down the handset and I know she's doing her best to think of new reasons I should change my number and forget all about Jonny Webb. Then she lets out a long sigh. "Bloody hell, Niamh, I can't believe you want to do this. You know I'm going to have to meet him, right?"

32
JONNY

I am a monster. I'm not sure even Iron Man would stoop this low and he's got a pretty shady track record where women are concerned.

And the worst thing is, what I told Niamh is only half a lie. Okay, the bit where I said she was the reason I first got in touch wasn't true but I do fancy her. I like her too, even when she's being all stroppy and sharp. She hides behind that attitude but underneath it she's not tough at all. And when we're messaging it feels like we have a connection; I don't want to lose that, which is another reason I couldn't tell her the truth. But mostly it's because the second I knew she was Leo's twin, I got scared about how she'd react to the truth. Knowing they were twins changes things; I don't know why but it does.

So I lied. I don't want to think about what Em would say if she knew what I've done, or that I've made things worse by arranging to see Niamh again – I have no plans to tell her about that either. She'd accuse me of using Niamh to get more information about Leo and I'd have to hold my hands up. But it's worse than that: if it turns out Leo is my donor then Em will tell me his twin is off-limits. And secretly, I think she might be right. Which makes what I've just done even scummier.

The trouble is I'm selfish – I want to keep seeing Niamh just as much as I need to know if this is Leo's heart. And that's my real problem: I'm not sure I can have both.

"Who do you think is gonna win the league?"

Marco's question prompts a furious response among the lads, some of which I understand and other parts I don't. It's break time and we're out in the freezing cold again, so that they can feed their nicotine habit. It doesn't freak me out so much any more – I've learned to sit upwind of them and most of the time they're a good laugh. The stuff they talk about is occasionally interesting, too – like this conversation, for instance. I know Leo was a Chelsea supporter because his mum arranged for a signed shirt to be auctioned as part of a fundraising night – it was all over the Facebook page. There are pictures of him wearing the Chelsea strip when he was a kid, too. So I've started paying attention whenever talk turns to football.

"Arsenal are never going to win it," Eavis says, scowling ferociously at Jackson. "Top four, maybe, but they're not champion material."

"Spurs ain't doing it either," Jackson fires back. "Their star striker can't score."

"Speaking of scoring, have you seen his missus?" Charlie cuts in. "Proper fit."

Eavis glances over at him scornfully. "Yeah, but you think Mrs Walsh is fit and she's older than my granny."

The others grunt with laughter and I join in, even though I've never thought of Mrs Walsh that way. Eavis and Charlie obviously have. It feels a little bit wrong – she probably has a husband and kids.

"Dunno what you're laughing at, Jonny," Eavis says suddenly, his piggy eyes fixed on me. "You're faulty goods, mate. I bet you've never even had a girlfriend."

That sends everyone else into gales of fresh laughter. "Good one, Eavis," Jackson says. "He wouldn't know what to do with a girl."

I feel my face starting to go red, embarrassment flooding into every cell of my body. Expectation mingles with the smoke – they're waiting for me to prove I'm one of them. I stare at the ground, trying to think of a comeback, willing the blood to leave my face. Then another thought creeps into my mind: what would Iron Man do in a situation like this? Would he let them laugh or would he take them down with a snappy one-liner? No, wait, what would *Leo* do? And in a flash of inspiration, I know what to say.

"That's not what your mum said, Jackson."

The stunned silence lasts for about 0.7 seconds, then the air is filled with a chorus of howls and jeers. Jackson looks like he wants to punch me but the others are pushing and shoving him so much he can't.

"Just banter, mate," I say, spreading my hands and looking innocent. "Just banter."

Charlie slaps me on the shoulder. "Legend, Jonny!"

Even Marco, who until this point has been watching events like a king surveying his subjects, laughs. "Good one, Jonno. Looks like you've got some balls after all."

I feel as though I've passed some kind of test, like I'm part of the group now. And I've got to admit it feels good to belong.

NIAMH

I have nothing to wear. Literally every item of clothing I own is spread out on the floor, the bed, the bedside table and there is nothing I want to put on. Well, I say nothing – I'm already wearing a pair of black skinny jeans and a long-sleeved top that covers the scaly patches on my elbows. In half an hour, I am supposed to meet Jonny outside the cinema in Hampstead Village and, at this rate, the film will be over by the time I get there.

"What about the Blondie T-shirt with your skinny jeans?" Helen says, lifting a screwed-up white bundle bearing the face of Debbie Harry from my bed.

I've wriggled halfway out of my top before I remember why I can't wear that shirt. "Leo flicked Bolognese sauce over it for a joke and the stains never washed out. It looks like she's got acne."

Helen inspects Debbie's face then drops the T-shirt onto the floor, sweeping up another in its place. "This?"

It's my *Rocky Horror Picture Show* shirt, from the time Uncle Pete decided our lives weren't complete until he'd taken Leo and me to a short-lived West End production a few years ago and Leo loaned me his pocket money to buy the T-shirt. It's so small now it barely covers my stomach but I can't bring myself to throw it away. "Too cold."

Helen looks around again. "How about this?" she says, pulling a football shirt from its hanger on the back of the door. "Old school."

The shirt she's holding up is Leo's – one from five or six seasons ago – that's been washed so many times the blue has faded and the Chelsea logo is so cracked it looks like Banksy painted it. I used to sleep in it, before the accident. Now I sometimes wear it under my clothes. So only I know it's there.

"Throw it over," I say, and catch it by the sleeve. Each time I wear it I expect to get a reminder of Leo's scent. But it smells faintly of washing powder, nothing more.

Helen checks her watch – for someone who doesn't want me to go and meet Jonny, she's eager to get out of the front door. But that's Helen – pathologically polite, even with people she's not keen on. I don't want to be late either, so after another millisecond's hesitation, I pull on the shirt. "Okay. How do I look?"

As she studies me, a reluctant smile tugs at her lips. "Happy," she says, shaking her head. "You look happy."

Now that she's said it, I realize she's right – I am happy, or as close as I ever get to happiness, anyway. There's a fizzy, excited feeling inside me, like I'm five years old and it's Christmas Eve. I probably shouldn't let myself feel like this but it's been so long since there was a break in the fog that I'll clutch at anything. "We should get going," I say, picking up my coat. "It'll take half an hour to get past the gatekeeper."

But it turns out I'm wrong. Mum's head is in fundraising mode and she lets us go with the bare minimum of fuss, although the weight of her anxious gaze still presses down on me as I pull on my coat. I have to text her when I get there, of course, and when I'm setting off home, but it's a long way from the usual third degree. Dad doesn't even look up from whatever History Channel show he's watching. Even so, I bundle Helen out of the door so fast she nearly trips over the doormat.

"Your dad was quiet," she says, as we hurry along to the bus stop. "Is he okay?"

I'm not sure how to answer. The truth is Dad is quiet these days but since I don't see much of him, it's easier not to notice how he's changed. I have noticed his hair though;

it's always been so black that Leo and I were sure he must dye it but it's turned salt-and-pepper grey now, like he's given up trying to stay young. I don't know what that means. Maybe it doesn't mean anything. "He's all right," I tell Helen. "It's Mum who's lost the plot."

She nods. "It doesn't seem right, lying to her. She wouldn't have stopped you going."

"Yeah, she would," I say. "We didn't lie, anyway – technically, we are going to the cinema. It's just the next bit we left out."

"That's called lying by omission," Helen says pointedly, reminding me she wants to be a lawyer and for approximately the millionth time, I wonder if I'm doing the right thing by bringing her along. If she starts cross-examining Jonny, I might rugby tackle her.

"Maybe, but what she doesn't know can't hurt her," I reply, as the bus pulls up. "Everyone lies to their parents, it's our job."

She presses her lips together, like she wants to argue but she can't because it's true – every single one of us lies to our parents about all kinds of stuff. *No, I don't have any homework... Yes, I'm revising... Of course I didn't eat junk for lunch... Yes, I went to my counselling session today...* There are things your family needs to know and there are things that are none of their business. Jonny is my secret. I don't know why it feels important to keep him to myself but it does. I want him to stay separate, in a little box away from the sadness and regret and wistfulness in the rest of my life. Teresa's eyes would light up if I told her that, which is another reason to keep it secret.

"Does he know I'm coming?" Helen asks, as the bus rumbles towards the high street.

"No," I answer. He knows who Helen is, of course; I talk about her a lot. He doesn't know what she thinks of him, though. I'm hoping that meeting him properly will change her opinion. I really hope she doesn't mention the stalking thing. It's one thing me and Jonny making jokes about it but I wouldn't want him to think I laugh about him with Helen behind his back.

I see him before he sees me. I'm weirdly nervous already, the skin around the edge of my thumbnail stings from where I've picked at it on the bus, but seeing him causes a horde of butterflies to batter my insides. If I was on my own, I might be tempted to text an excuse and go home, which I suppose is another reason it's good to have Helen here – she doesn't run away from anything and is dragging me along behind her like one of those toy dogs on a string Leo and I used to fight over when we were little. And underneath my nerves, I really, really want to see him, especially because I know he really wants to see me.

I catch up with Helen. "You are going to be nice, aren't you?"

"Of course I am," she says, rolling her eyes. "When am I ever not nice?"

I glance over at Jonny, hoping he isn't going to think I'm strange for bringing Helen. But it's too late to back out – he's seen us. "Come on," I mutter. "Let's get this over with."

He looks confused as we approach him. "All right?" He nods, his gaze flickering from me to Helen and back again.

"Yeah," I say, not sure how to explain without offending him. "This is Helen. She wanted to meet you."

He stares at me for a second, then shrugs. "Okay. Hi, Helen."

"Hi," Helen replies coolly. "I just wanted to check you're not an axe murderer."

"Helen!" I cry, mortified beyond belief. "Shut up!"

Jonny laughs and glances over at me. "Why would you think that?"

"You know what they say about people you meet online," Helen says, unsmiling. "You can never be sure they're who they say they are."

"Helen!" I say again, throwing her a pleading look she ignores. "Stop."

Still amused, Jonny raises one eyebrow. "I'm Jonny Webb and I'm fifteen. I go to St Albans College and support Chelsea. I don't own an axe and I've never killed anything, apart from flies and the occasional joke. What else do you want to know?"

I glance at Helen and I know she's thinking of the shirt I've got on under my coat. Jonny's going to think I wore it for him, even though I'm pretty sure I had no idea which team he supported. But her gaze flicks back to Jonny, a little frown creasing her forehead like she's working him out. Then she shakes her head and purses her lips. "Nothing," she says. "For now. Text me if you need me – I'll be in Nando's with my parents."

That last comment is aimed at me but the implication that she doesn't trust Jonny clangs in my ears. With a brisk nod at him, she walks away. Part of me wants to go with her – how can I even look at Jonny after that?

"So that was…weird," he says. "Is she always like that?"

"What, like a mini version of my mother?" I sigh and shake my head. "No, she's not."

He hesitates and looks away. "It's okay. She's just looking out for you."

I know he's right, which is why I don't really feel cross with Helen. She could have been a bit less obvious but this whole situation was awkward – maybe the direct approach was the best one. And she's gone now, anyway, leaving me alone with Jonny for the next few hours. Jonny who says he likes me…Jonny who I like quite a lot too. "We should probably go in," I say.

Nodding, he heads towards the door. "Does Helen know which film we're going to see?"

"No, and I'm not going to tell her," I say, glancing at the black and red slasher poster. "If she ever asks, we went to see *Pandas on Parade*, okay?"

He grins and goes inside. I hold back for a moment, watching the way he walks, and my phone vibrates in my pocket. It's a message from Helen.

Jury's out, it says.

34

JONNY

I shouldn't have come.

It's great to see Niamh again, although she looked like she might throw up when she first arrived, and Helen scared the crap out of me. Even now she's gone and we're sitting in the dark of the cinema, I can still remember her rock-hard stare. She knows I'm lying, I think, even though it's not possible for her to know. She's added me on Facebook too, probably so she can investigate more, and I'm glad I created my new, clean account. But that's not why I should have stayed away.

I've searched and searched for possible donors. It has to be a certain kind of death to allow the organs to be eligible for transplant and there aren't any others that fit. So I'm

99.99% sure there's only one possible person my heart could have come from: Leo. And there's no way I should be on a date with his twin. I should stop things now, break it to her gently once the film is over. But I can see her face, lit by the glow from the screen, and I like the cute way her nose turns up at the end, the tendrils of hair escaping from her ponytail, the little lines of concentration between her eyes as she watches the story unfold. I like that she hasn't dressed up to meet me and still looks fit, especially since the blue of her shirt brings out the colour of her eyes. The trouble is, she's also Leo's sister – I can't let myself feel any of this.

The film isn't up to much; a lot of screaming and fake blood can't make up for the terrible acting. There's a half-empty carton of popcorn between Niamh and me; the smell is driving me mad. I've already eaten more than I should, although not as much as Niamh – I can imagine Em waving a finger at me, telling me to step away from the snacks. She definitely wouldn't approve of the vat of Coke in the cup holder next to me. Or maybe she would. When we planned our trip to the cinema for our Unbucket list, back when we were both sick, stuffing down the unhealthiest snacks we could find was pretty high on the agenda. That seems like a long time ago now. Once Em's fought off this infection, I'm going to remind her of that plan. We'll see a better film than this one, though.

The next time I look at Niamh, she's watching me. She doesn't look away either, so we sit there staring at each other, ignoring the rising body count, ignoring everything. I have no idea what she's thinking but the feeling I'm getting is pretty intense. One of her eyebrows is slightly higher than the other, making her look as though she's asking me a question. Every now and then, her eyes flick down to my mouth and I realize our heads have moved closer together. If I wanted to kiss her, I reckon I could. She'd taste of salty popcorn and sugary drinks and now I've thought of it, there's nothing I want to do more. My heart thuds in my chest so loudly I'm sure everyone must be able to hear it. And that's when I remember who she is, why I can't kiss her or even think about her that way. Reluctantly, I tear my gaze away and fix it on the screen. After a second or two, I sense she does the same and the moment disappears.

35

NIAMH

29 October 01:20

Let's run away.

The message comes through as I'm shivering outside Leo's door, listening to the muffled sobs coming from inside. I ought to go in and comfort her, cuddle her as though I'm the parent and she's the child, tell her everything's going to be all right. Except that we both know it isn't. The best we can hope is that it won't always be this hard. At the very least I should go and wake Dad but there's nothing he can do either and then there'll be three of us awake and miserable. I wonder briefly about getting the packet of antidepressants that are still down the back of my bed, gathering dust, but I don't think that's the answer either. So I stand there for another helpless minute and then trudge back to bed, my head aching with held-back tears.

I jam in my earbuds and smile in spite of myself when I read the message again – Jonny told me he was going to sleep over an hour ago and I like that he's still awake, thinking about me.

01:25
You read my mind. Where to?

The suggestion is more appealing than he could possibly know. Mum had come out of her fundraising cave by the time I'd got home from the cinema and was standing fretfully by the front window, curtain pulled back, staring out. Dad was nowhere to be seen. I gritted my teeth, endured the fussing, then fled before her anxiety destroyed what was left of my good mood. And then I lay on my bed, gazing up at the ceiling, remembering how it felt to sit next to Jonny, our knees touching in the dark. There was one moment when I caught him watching me, like he was trying to figure out what I was feeling. I don't know what he saw but he looked away a few seconds later. Maybe he was thinking about kissing me. I wish he had.

01:31

I don't know. Somewhere sunny, where it's just you
and me. Brighton, maybe? In the morning, for the day.

Brighton is on the coast, I think uneasily – I haven't
been near the sea since Leo's accident. But the idea of
escaping is good and the thought of getting away with
Jonny is even better. I don't want him to think I've got
some kind of weird beach phobia. Or worse, that it's him
I'm trying to avoid.

It'll be okay, I decide. It's not as though we're going
back to the beach where it happened. And if Mum asks, I'll
tell her I'm studying over at Helen's. Even she can't moan
about that.

01:34

Sounds like a plan, Ghoul-Boy. What time?

We meet at Victoria Station. It's quiet, full of weekend
travellers instead of commuters, lingering around the shops.
Jonny's early, as always. His designer-label dependency
makes me want to eye roll, but I still think about kissing
him hello.

"Tell me," I say as soon as I'm in earshot, "did you hear
a *baaaa* when you looked in the mirror this morning?"

"Hello, Niamh," he replies evenly. "Not that I noticed. Why?"

I wave a hand at his clothes. "Because you're clearly a label-junkie and nothing you're wearing says 'I am Jonny'."

He looks uncomfortable, making me think I've hit a nerve. "I like this stuff."

"Huh," I reply. "Labels are for people who don't know what they like."

Jonny studies my clothes. "And black is the new blah."

I'm not offended, because he's right. I wear black because it's easy and I can't be bothered to find anything else. But the truth is, it took me twenty minutes to put together this exact outfit and fifteen more to add my perfectly flicked black eyeliner and mascara. I don't admit that, though. "Black suits me, or hadn't you noticed?"

He tilts his head to one side and looks at me for so long that I get squiggles in my stomach. "I noticed."

Flustered, I peer up at the departures board. "There's a train at nine-fifty. Shall we get that one?"

"Sounds good," he says. "The ticket machines are over there."

We squabble briefly over who is paying – he insisted on buying the tickets and snacks at the cinema and I'm determined to assert my equality today. After a minute of intense discussion, Jonny steps back, shaking his head. "You don't like being taken care of, do you?"

"I don't like being patronized," I fire back.

"I'm not trying to patronize you. I'm trying to be ro— nice."

His cheeks flush and he looks away. He was going to say romantic, I know he was. And although I feel bad for stopping him, there's something we need to get straight. "Listen, Jonny, the last thing I need is someone else telling me what to do, how to act. If that's what you want then I'm going home."

His eyes widen. "No! God, no, that's not what I want at all. I've had a lifetime of being told what to do. I'd never pull the same crap on someone else."

And there it is again; that hint that there's plenty he's not telling me. I watch him for a moment, wondering what his secrets are. "Good," I say, taking some money out of my pocket. "If it makes you feel better, you can buy me some chips when we get there."

He's quiet as we settle into our seats. It's not until the train starts moving that he speaks again. "Have you ever woken up in the morning and wondered who you are?"

"How d'you mean?"

He gazes out of the window at the greyness of London as it flashes by. "Obviously not your name. But have you ever taken a long hard look at yourself and realized you're seeing a stranger, someone you don't know at all?"

Mostly, I see echoes of Leo – in my lips, the shape of my

nose, my eyes – but I don't say that. Instead, I think of all the times we argued. Mum used to tell me we weren't always like that – we were best friends once – but it changed as we grew up. He'd accuse me of being a wannabe goth and I'd scream back that he was a Poundshop Kurt Cobain. But for all the insults and arguments, for better or worse, I always knew who I was: Niamh Brody, Leo's twin. When he died, I lost that link – lost my sense of being one half of a whole, part of a pair. I'm not anyone's sister any more. I'm on my own.

Swallowing hard, I push the feeling of loss away. "Maybe. Why?"

"You accused me of being a sheep," he says. "I didn't realize until you said it but you're right – I do wear this stuff because everyone else does. I don't know who Abercrombie and Fitch even are. But it's more than that." He runs a hand through his hair and takes a deep breath. "Something happened to me before I met you, something that meant I didn't have a normal childhood, the kind that shapes who you become when you grow up. So I don't have a – a style or a thing that's essentially me but please don't judge me for it. The labels are just a place holder, something I'm using until I work a few things out."

Silence fills the air, punctuated by the clickety-clack of the train as it speeds along. I kind of like that he's a little bit broken – it evens things up between us. And I'm desperate to ask what happened to make him this way but I think he'd have told me if he wanted me to know. And the weird thing is, I get what he's saying: black is my label, the thing I hide behind. The sheep comment was low and I wish I could take it back.

"Nobody knows who Abercrombie and Fitch are," I say. "But for what it's worth, whoever you want to be is fine with me."

He nods, his gaze fixed on the window. Slowly, I lean forward and place my elbow on the table, holding up a hand and spreading my fingers in the air. He hesitates long enough for a blush to creep up my cheeks, then he looks into my eyes and one by one, his fingertips touch mine. We sit that way for a moment, a mirror image, until Jonny shifts his fingers to one side, sliding them between mine and curling them around so that he's holding my hand. A second later, I do the same.

We stay like that all the way to Brighton.

It's a bright, clear day on the coast, with a sky the colour of sapphires. We walk out of the bustling, noisy station to the sound of seagulls crying and the shrill beep of a taxi as an oblivious hen party steps inadvertently into its path. There's a faint tang of salt in the air, which immediately makes my stomach clench. *Get a hold of yourself, Brody.*

"Which way?" I ask with a shiver that has nothing to do with the cool breeze.

Jonny consults his phone. "Straight on to the seafront. Or down a bit and left to the Lanes."

"The Lanes?" I repeat, wondering if it's some kind of bowling alley.

"Shops," he explains. "Vintage shops. I thought you could help me find some new clothes."

"Maybe," I say, setting off down the road. "It depends how you like black."

Although I only chose to go there so that we wouldn't head straight to the beach, the Lanes are actually pretty cool. We spend an hour roaming up and down the narrow streets, ducking in and out of the quirky little boutiques. By the time we hit the last shop, Jonny has four new T-shirts and a pair of vintage Levi's so worn they fit like a second skin. He turns to me, holding up a Nirvana T-shirt. "What do you think?"

"Nah," I say, rattling through another rail. "Leo's thing, not mine."

He doesn't reply and when we go to pay, I see the T-shirt peeking out from underneath the skull one I picked out. God, I hope he's not another Cobain wannabe.

"What now?" he says, as we pick our way through the crowds and emerge into an empty side street. "Hungry?"

He pulls out his phone just as it buzzes. The expression

on his faces changes as he looks at it and he stuffs it back into his pocket. "Actually, I could do with finding a toilet."

I'm soon lost in the warren of streets but Jonny has an app and seems to know where he's going. I follow, trying to shift the growing sense of panic in my head. I was fine when we were shopping but now I can hear the faint sound of the sea and it's making me shake. I slow down, fighting to control my breathing; oblivious, Jonny goes on ahead. He vanishes around a corner, making me even more anxious, and I speed up, only to be met by the sight of greeny-brown waves ahead. A sudden gust of wind buffets me, filling my lungs with briny sea air – we've reached the seafront. The salt hits the back of my throat, making me gag, and I know I've made a huge mistake: I'm not ready to face the beach yet. Both hands fly to my mouth as bile rises up in my throat and dread squeezes at my heart. The waves roar, crashing against the stones, and I'm back on the beach in Devon. A high-pitched wail fills the air, thin and anguished. For a moment, I stand there frozen, the blood pounding in my ears. Then, without so much as a glance at Jonny, I turn tail and run.

"Niamh!"

She stops screaming and is running before I have a chance to work out what's wrong, turning the corner and tearing away from me at a surprising speed. I have no choice but to follow. And as we race along the uneven streets, I guess what the problem is: the beach. I bet it's the first time she's been near one since Leo's death. Which makes it even more important that I catch her.

It's a good few minutes before she slows to a walk, by which time we've left the sea behind us and have reached the Royal Pavilion Gardens. It's the most exercise I've done in for ever and I'm out of breath but grateful to find that's all. She comes to a stop among the flower beds, shoulders heaving and cheeks pink from the exertion.

"Sorry," she says, when I reach her, puffing and panting. "I couldn't…"

She trails off, her eyes glistening with tears. I point to a nearby bench. "Want to sit down?"

I wait while she catches her breath, thankful for the chance to catch my own, and gaze at the flowers around us, trying to ignore the questions buzzing in my brain. If she wants to explain, she will. At the back of my mind is the message from my mum, reminding me to take my medication but the pills will have to wait. All I care about right now is Niamh.

"You must think I'm an idiot," she says, her eyes not meeting mine.

"Nah," I say. "I'm actually pretty impressed. You put the lads I play football with to shame."

She almost smiles. Almost. "I didn't expect it to get me like that. But the noise – the smell – it was just—"

She breaks off and swallows hard. I should say something reassuring here, about how grief affects us all differently but everything I come up with sounds like it comes straight from my counsellor. So I stay quiet and listen.

"He'd think it was hilarious, seeing me in such a state," she goes on, wrapping her arms around herself. "Leo loved to laugh."

I hold my breath, hoping she doesn't stop talking, for

her sake even more than mine. Because it seems as though she's overwhelmed by her anger and grief and she needs to let some of it out. She shakes her head. "Even now, he's everywhere I look."

"I bet you miss him."

She stares down at her fingers. "You'd think so, wouldn't you? But actually, I hate him. It was his fault we climbed the stupid rocks in the first place. I would never have risked it if he hadn't dared me."

I'd always assumed it was too hard for her to talk much about what happened but it's obvious I've got that wrong. She doesn't talk about Leo because she can't, not without stirring up all kinds of other feelings, the kind other people wouldn't understand. "It helps to have someone to blame, right?"

"Yeah," she says, glancing up at me in surprise. "It did help, for a while. But I can't tell anyone how I really feel, especially not the useless counsellor they make me see. I can't say a bad word about tragic Saint Leo, saviour of the sick."

The words slam into me like a truck. "Saviour of the sick?" I repeat slowly, wondering if she means what I think she means.

She lets out a short laugh. "Oh yeah, didn't you know? He wanted his organs to be donated when he died. Ever the superstar, that's my brother." Then she rubs her face with both hands. "Sorry. You don't need me dumping all this crap on you."

"It's okay," I say, rubbing her arm as what I already suspected becomes real. I take a long slow breath in, feeling the blood pumping through my veins, and exhale shakily. It has to be Leo's heart inside me. There's no way it could be anyone else's, the chances are too slim. But as much as I feel like I should come clean, this isn't the time to spring it on Niamh. What she needs now is a friend, not someone with their own agenda. Unluckily for her, all she has is me. "Really, I don't mind."

She sighs. "But I do. I came here to get away from him, not to bore you with my problems."

Standing up, I take both her hands. "You're never boring. The opposite, in fact."

She looks at me quizzically then, her head angled upwards, her cheeks flushing again and I realize she's not used to being listened to, not used to getting compliments. I make a mental note to give her more. And that's when I know for sure I've been fooling myself – I started off wanting to find out more about Leo but it's been all about Niamh since – well, almost since I met her. And the thought thrills me and terrifies me at the same time because I know I shouldn't go there, I shouldn't see her again. It isn't fair to either of us. The trouble is, I'm not sure I can give her up now.

I tug on her hands, meaning to pull her to her feet but she's lighter than I expect and I pull too hard. She flies upwards and crashes into my chest with a startled squeak. And now that she's there, pressed against me, it feels like the most natural thing in the world to put my arms around her and kiss her. At least, that's what I want to do. I think she wants me to do it too – her lips part and she's looking at me in a way that makes me suddenly breathless. But in between the thinking and the doing, I wait too long and she steps backwards before I can drop my mouth to hers.

There's an awkward silence. "You must be desperate for the loo by now," she says.

And that's it: the moment is officially killed. I smile wryly, because there's nothing else I can do. "A bit. Shall we go and get a drink?"

NIAMH

I don't get it. It felt like Jonny was going to kiss me when we were outside that incredible, ridiculous pavilion and I thought he might have tried it on the train home, when we had the carriage practically to ourselves but he sat in the seat opposite and kept a respectable distance between us the whole time, not even holding my hand. And now we're walking along Hampstead High Street, he's barely talking to me and I don't know what I've done wrong. He keeps fidgeting, checking his watch, like he can't wait to get away from me. It was all that crap about Leo – it must have freaked him out. He didn't seem bothered at the time but maybe he's had time to think about it now and has decided I'm too messed up. Too broken. Brilliant.

We reach the bus stop and sit in silence for a while, our breath making clouds in the freezing night air. I should tell him to go, I'll be fine, but I know he'll insist on staying, even though it's clear he'd rather be anywhere else. People wander past, a few stop and wait for the next bus, and I wonder what they make of us, obviously together but not speaking. Jonny stares into the distance, avoiding my gaze and I feel another stab of bewilderment. Maybe it's got nothing to do with Leo – Jonny might just be shy. Maybe he's never kissed anyone and doesn't know how to start; I'm not sure I do, come to think of it. Or maybe he's waiting for some kind of sign from me that it's okay. So I take a deep breath and reach out to take his hand.

His head whips around to look at me and I see surprise in his eyes. Surprise coupled with something else. "Niamh—" he starts to say, a warning note in his voice but I don't let him finish. Instead, I lean across and plant my mouth firmly on his.

After a heartbeat, I feel his lips soften and move against mine. His mouth opens and a thrill rushes through me – he does want to. One of my hands creeps up and touches the back of his neck, brushing the fine hair there. A second later, everything changes. His eyes snap open and he pushes me away. "I can't do this," he croaks. "It's – I – sorry, I just can't."

He stands up and walks off, leaving me rooted to the

spot, shock freezing me to my core. And then the heat of humiliation sears the cold away and tears prickle my eyes. I'm so stupid – he didn't want to kiss me at all. And by forcing him, I've ruined everything.

There's a snigger somewhere behind me, followed by a thud. I glance around to see a boy frowning, and rubbing his arm and a girl looking apologetically my way. Furiously, I huddle deeper into my coat, willing myself not to cry. I've done too much of that already.

Getting to my feet, I stumble over to the late-night mini-market and wander aimlessly round until I see the painkillers behind the checkout. I buy a pack and wash two down on my way back to the bus stop. I know they won't help but I swallow them anyway.

Anything's worth a shot tonight.

38 JONNY

"Nice T-shirt," Marco says as we slouch along the corridor on Monday. "I didn't know you were into Nirvana."

I hesitate, because I've only listened to a few tracks so far. I like what I've heard, though. I can see why Leo was such a fan. "Yeah, they're good."

"How was your weekend?" he goes on.

The question catches me by surprise. I look at him hard, wondering if he's going to follow up with some kind of put-down but there's genuine interest on his face. "Not bad, thanks."

"Did you watch the match?" he asks. "Barcelona were good but I reckon Real Madrid have got their name on the La Liga trophy already."

I nod distractedly – now he mentions it, I remember him talking about it last week. Another time I might ask him about it but not today. Today, I can't go for more than five minutes without thinking about Niamh and replaying the way her face crumpled when I pushed her away last night. I really want to talk to Em about it, in an "asking for a friend" kind of way, but she hasn't answered my last message yet. Which leaves me with Marco – who knows what dubious wisdom he'll come up with?

I fire a sideways glance his way as we walk into business. "Listen, can I ask you something?"

"Depends what it is."

I pause, wondering if I'm about to make a mistake, then lower my voice. "There's this girl I've been seeing…"

He stops and stares at me, a slow grin spreading over his face. "You kept that quiet, you dirty dog."

I look around to see if anyone is listening. Nobody is showing the slightest interest. "It's early days. The thing is, it's a bit complicated. She – uh – kissed me recently and I…well, I pushed her away."

The grin fades. "Are you trying to tell me you're gay?"

"No!"

Marco regards me suspiciously. "Is she ugly, then?"

"No," I repeat, a mental image of Niamh floating into

my head. "She's gorgeous. Like I said, it's a bit complicated."

"I don't see how," Marco says, starting to walk again. "Sounds like she was well up for it and you blew her out, for no apparent reason."

I'm starting to wish I'd kept quiet. "Just forget it."

"Seems to me you're overthinking it," Marco says, throwing his bag onto the table and sliding into his seat. "If she's fit and willing, get in there. And if she's ugly, close your eyes and think of someone else."

The girl on the next table – Isabel, I think she's called – throws both of us dirty looks. I can't say I blame her – Marco is being a pig and I'm guilty by association. But he's oblivious to her disgust and drops her a broad wink. "I'd keep my eyes open for you, sweetheart."

Her nose wrinkles in horror and she turns her back. Marco shrugs, outwardly unruffled but I catch a flicker of disappointment in his eyes, like he was hoping she'd take him up on the offer or something. And if that's true then he knows even less about girls than I do. I pick up my pen and start doodling on the back of my notepad – a girl with a heart-shaped face and hurt-filled eyes. Maybe Marco's got a point about Niamh, to be honest – I could be overthinking things. Let's face it, she's single, I'm single, she's not related to me in any way – it just so happens that her dead brother's heart is now mine. If I take that fact out of the equation, then there's nothing standing in our way

– she's just a girl who apparently fancies me and I'm just a boy who definitely fancies her. Who says I even have to tell her about Leo's heart? Especially since the official line is I'm not supposed to know.

Everyone has secrets, right?

The lads go to the park for a kick-about after school. I trail along after them and stand next to their pile of bags and coats, watching them play. At least it gives me something to do; Niamh hasn't replied to my text or the Facebook message I sent earlier, asking for a chance to explain. I don't know what I'm going to say if she replies, or even if she will reply, but I'll think of something. Because the more I think about it, the more I wish I hadn't stopped her from kissing me. It's been on my mind all day, how good it felt, where it might have led. But it's more than that – what I want most is to wipe away the hurt I saw in her eyes when I pulled away. She's had a terrible time over the last few months. The last thing she needs is someone like me making her feel worse. Someone with a secret like mine.

"Oi, Jonny!" Jackson's shout snaps me out of my thoughts and back into the park. "Get the ball!"

I look around and see the ball some distance away. Jogging over to it, I'm about to pick it up when it occurs to me that I might be able to join in the game now. I am supposed to exercise and it's just a kick-about with a bunch of lads. Who knows, maybe some of Leo's skills with the ball will have rubbed off on me.

Twenty minutes later, I'm prepared to admit they have not. The others are much better than me; most of them are faster with the ball in spite of their smoke-clogged lungs and what they lack in speed, they make up for in commitment. I lose count of the number of times I clatter to the ground, winded by the kind of tackle that would get a red card if we had a referee.

"Sorry, mate," Jackson says, smiling insincerely as he pulls me to my feet. "Thought I'd got the ball."

By the time we stop playing, I think I've improved a bit. We're all out of breath but while I gulp in lungfuls of clean air, Marco and his mates light up cigarettes. I cough pointedly and move upwind. Marco just grins and throws his empty cigarette packet at me. It bounces off my chest and lands directly in the path of a young woman pushing a pram. She scowls furiously in my direction and I reach down to pick it up, muttering a hasty apology as I stuff it into my pocket. Jackson watches her walk past and lets out a wolf whistle. "I would," he announces, loud enough for the words to carry.

She doesn't stop, shows no sign she's heard even though she must have. It bothers me the way they talk about women like they're not people at all, just bodies. They'd punch anyone who talked about their mum or sisters like that. But they don't seem to make the connection. I can't imagine Leo acting that way – football captain Leo definitely wasn't short of female attention. I could do worse than model Jonny 2.0 on him.

"Shut up, Jackson," I say, picking up my bag with a grunt of disgust.

Immediately, he's next to me, thrusting his sweaty face close to mine. "You going to make me, then?"

Old Jonny would have backed down, no question, but I'm not him any more. I've got Leo's heart and memory to live up to so I square my shoulders and stare back at him. "Face it, mate, it's all talk with you."

"I don't see you exactly beating the girls off with a stick," he scoffs. "I'm pretty sure the only thing you beat off is—"

"Jonny's got a girlfriend," Marco puts in mildly. "Or is it a boyfriend?"

I feel the heat start to rise in my cheeks and force myself to stay cool. "Girlfriend," I say, as my phone buzzes in my hand. "That'll be her now, in fact. See you later."

I walk away, deliberately not checking my phone until I'm safely out of sight. When I do look at the screen, I'm disappointed: one from Mum, wondering what time I'll be home and one out of the blue from Em.

17:01
When are you coming to see me? E x

Nothing from Niamh.
Maybe me and Jackson aren't so different after all.

NIAMH

Helen doesn't look smug when I tell her about Jonny. She doesn't pull faces or threaten to smash his stupid face into a thousand bits the way I wanted to last night. She doesn't even mention that I went to Brighton with him without telling her, while pretending to my mum that I was with her. Instead, she listens while I pour out the whole embarrassing tale at lunchtime.

"He just ran off and left you there? And he didn't give you any explanation?" she says when I finish.

"No," I reply moodily, scowling at a passing Year Seven boy. "He messaged to say he wants to explain. But it's obvious what the problem is, isn't it? He's got a girlfriend."

Her forehead wrinkles in confusion. "Who?"

"That Emily girl, the one who messaged me and told me to give him a chance," I say, trying not to sniff. "I asked him about her and he said they were just friends but there must be more to it."

Helen looks even more confused. "But it doesn't make sense. Why would she get in touch with you if she was seeing him?"

I shred the remains of my sandwich packet. "I don't know. Maybe they weren't together then. The only other reason I can think of is that he didn't really like me at all but I don't think that was it. Why go to all the trouble of contacting me if he wasn't interested?" I slump onto the table, face buried in my arms. "Why say all that stuff to me if he didn't mean it? Unless I freaked him out when I went off on one about Leo."

Helen sounds sympathetic. "It won't be that and if it is, then he's an insensitive idiot and you deserve better. Actually, whatever it is, you deserve better."

I'm not sure she's right – do I deserve better? I'm moody, sarcastic and occasionally flip out about my dead brother.

Why would anyone be interested in me?

I struggle through Tuesday but by Wednesday, I can't face the thought of school. I pretend to have a migraine and then sleep until mid-afternoon, which also means I miss an appointment with Teresa. Mum believes my headache story at first but when I won't get up on Thursday, she calls Helen. I hear them murmuring outside my bedroom door early on Friday, try to pretend I don't notice the door opening, ignore Helen's impatient demands that I get out of bed.

"Fine," she says, when I show no sign of moving. "I'll wait."

I can hear her turning the pages of a book. Then she starts to rummage around on the floor, picking things up and dropping them one after another. She's smart. She knows it's only a matter of time before I crack.

"What are you doing?" I snap, when she starts poking around under my bed. It's not that I have anything to hide… Not under the bed, anyway. The tablets are under my pillow, unopened for now. Surreptitiously, I fluff the pillow, making sure there's nothing showing.

"I'm not letting you do this," she says, sitting back and giving me a matter-of-fact look.

"You're not letting me do what – sleep?"

"I'm not letting you feel bad about something that isn't your fault." Her tone softens. "I know you're hurt but I'm pretty sure Jonny isn't putting himself through this."

I don't answer. What she's saying makes sense but it doesn't worry me how Jonny feels. I can only deal with how I feel, and right now the darkness is so heavy that it flattens me. "I can't sleep at night," I mumble. "And then when it's time to get up for school, I can't do it."

"Your mum is really worried," Helen says. "She reckons you're not eating much."

I pull back the duvet then, to reveal a jumble of empty crisp packets and chocolate wrappers. "Since when did my mother know anything about me?"

Helen stares at the mess for a long time without speaking. Then she folds her arms. "What you need is a reminder of how it feels to be alive. Let's go and watch the fireworks on Parliament Hill tomorrow night."

I burrow into the pillow and shut my eyes – I'd forgotten it's Bonfire Night. "No."

"There's a funfair on the heath," she says persuasively.

"I suppose it might be a laugh," I say slowly. "Mum won't let me go on the rides, though. She's been calling them deathtraps since before Leo died."

Helen smiles and stands up. "What was it you said the other day? What she doesn't know won't hurt her."

"It won't make me go back to school," I warn her.

She shrugs. "I'll come round at six. Wrap up warm."

I pull the duvet over my head to hide the smile I can't prevent. "Yes, Mum."

* * *

217

Parliament Hill is the best place to watch fireworks. It's like standing in the middle of the Big Bang, with booms and explosions of colour everywhere you look. It's especially good when you've had half a bottle of your parents' vodka to take the edge off things. Helen is shocked at first, then disapproving, but she has a few sips when I call her boring. I have to drink most of her share though, which is why I am teetering on the edge of a park bench, pretending to do karate while everyone around us glowers at me.

"Get down!" Helen says, tugging at my sleeve. "People are staring."

I want to shout that I don't care what they think but I can't actually be bothered so I half jump, half fall off the bench and sit heavily beside her. "I like fireworks."

Helen nods. "Me too." Her eyes narrow as I lift the vodka bottle to my lips again and she pulls it down before I can drink. "Let's save some for later."

"Spoilsport," I say, pouting.

By the time the best of the displays are over, I'm feeling pretty unsteady and need Helen's arm linked through mine as we make our way down to the funfair. The lights and noise blur before my eyes and even in my drunken state, I know the waltzers are a bad idea and not just because of my mother's warnings.

"We could go on the dodgems," I say, slurring a little.

"Is it illegal to be drunk in charge of a dodgem?"

Helen looks amused, her face weirdly psychedelic in the flashing lights of the rides. "Probably."

"You can drive then." I shake my head, sniffing the salty-sweet air. "Actually, forget the dodgems. I want to be drunk in charge of a hot dog instead."

"Let's walk around a bit first," Helen says, tugging me towards the garish stalls stuffed with oversized teddies and knock-off Disney toys. I wait until she's trying a hoopla game and then sneak a mouthful of vodka. She gives it a few more goes and I cheer her on, swigging down more drink when she's not looking. She doesn't win a thing. By the time we reach the food stalls, my head is beginning to spin and a hot dog is the last thing I want.

Helen sighs when she looks at me. "I can't take you home like this – your mum will freak."

I offer her the bottle. "Have some more. Then we'll both be in trouble."

She laughs and takes the vodka from my hand. "Nice try but one of us has to be sober." She drops it into an overflowing bin and drags me towards the exit. "Come on, let's hope the walk home sorts you out."

"Hey," I protest but my heart's not really in it. I don't want to admit it but I'm starting to feel a bit sick. The last thing I want is another drink.

We're halfway down the road when my pocket buzzes

and vibrates. I pull out my phone and wait for the screen to come into focus. "It's Jonny."

Helen scowls. "Again? Hasn't he got the message yet?"

"He can't get the message – I haven't sent him any," I say, peering at the dancing words. "He wants to talk."

She lets out a derisive snort and starts walking again. "Ask him when he was planning to tell you about his girlfriend."

I should, I think, as the words swirl around my alcohol-soaked brain. He came to me. He wanted to get to know me and the moment I let him get close, he ran away. A flame of hard-edged anger bursts into life. I deserve some kind of explanation and I'm tempted to answer now and demand one. But another idea is trying to get my attention; it's easy to weasel out of things on the phone and come up with plausible-sounding excuses. What I really need to do is look Jonny in the eye and ask what he's playing at, why he thinks it's okay to mess with people's heads and lead them on and make them feel things they wouldn't have felt otherwise – especially when those people might be struggling with a whole world of other stuff.

The anger coalesces into solid fury, a hard lump in the pit of my stomach. What I want to know most is why he started all this in the first place.

I reach out and grip Helen's arm tightly, forcing her to stop. "Want to do something crazy?"

"No," she says, her face wary in the orangey street light. "I want to walk you home before you get into any more trouble."

"Let's go to St Albans instead."

A look of panicky understanding crosses her face. "That's a really bad idea, Niamh. You don't even know where he lives."

I wave an airy hand. "I'll ring him from the station, make him come meet us. And when he shows up I'll tell him what a tosser he is and then we can go home."

She frowns. "Does he live near the station? How big is St Albans?"

I hesitate because I don't actually know the answer to either question, but the idea of going feels so right that I don't want to think about the details. "Smaller than London, and it's not far from here," I say, but she still doesn't look convinced. "Come on, it'll make me feel better. Isn't that what tonight's all about?"

"Don't pull that emotional-blackmail stuff on me," Helen says, taking my hand and pulling me along the road again. "If you really want to see him, do it when you're sober."

I blink at her. "But I won't want to see him when I'm sober."

"Problem solved," she says. "You'll thank me in the morning."

I take a few more steps, then stop in the middle of the pavement and yank my hand from hers. "I'm going to see him."

"No, Niamh," she says in her most Helen tone of voice. "No, you're not."

"I am," I insist. "I am going to St Albans to tell Jonny exactly what he can do with his stupid teddy bear. Come on, Hel, let's have an adventure!"

Helen stares at me for a long time, like she's trying to work out how to defuse me. Then she lets out a little sigh of defeat. "I want you to remember this was all your idea."

I nod a bit too fervently – her face goes out of focus. "Okay," I say. "I'll remember. Can we go now?"

She shakes her head and loops her arm through mine. "No. If you're going to drag me to deepest St Albans then I'm going to need a hot dog for the journey."

I'm listening to Nirvana, wondering which song was Leo's favourite, and idly picking out a few chords Dad taught me on his old acoustic guitar when Niamh rings. After seven days of total silence, I was starting to believe I'd blown it and now she's ringing me at ten o'clock at night. Even so, I wait as long as I dare before I pick up.

"Hi," I say, trying to sound cool. "What's up?"

Whatever I'm expecting, it's not the blast of incoherent mumbling and whining I get. "What?"

She starts talking again and this time I make out a few more words. I can hear someone else in the background too, a female voice that sounds like Helen, although she's a lot less slurred. I stifle a groan. "Have you been drinking?"

Now Niamh is mumbling something else. I should hang up and call her back in the morning, when she's sober, but she probably won't answer the phone. This might be the only chance I get. "Niamh, I can't understand you."

She seems to make an effort to speak more clearly because suddenly I catch every word. "You're a knob, Jonny Webb."

I smile in spite of the insult. "Yeah. Sorry."

"Helen thinks you owe me an explanation and I think she's right." The words tumble out so fast that I have to really concentrate to get what she's saying. "You can't just go around making people kiss you and then being a dick about it."

There's a tap on my door and Dad pokes his head round, making the universal sign for tea. I shake my head with a frown, wondering about the muffled loudspeaker announcement in the background. "Where are you?" I say, as Dad pulls the door shut.

"We're in St Albans, obviously."

The last word drips with typical Niamh scorn. I think about looking out of the window – they can't be outside, Niamh doesn't know my address. Even so, I twitch the curtain to one side. "Where?"

There's a muffled conversation and some thuds which sound a lot like two people wrestling over the phone. Then Niamh speaks again, slightly out of breath. "Outside the station. They kicked us out of the waiting room and Helen wants to go home."

I have a sudden image of the local community support officers reeling Niamh in for underage drinking. "Stay there," I say, reaching for my rucksack. "I'm on my way."

They're exactly where I expect them to be, sitting on a bench near to the empty bike racks. Helen is talking animatedly to Niamh, who has her head down, gaze fixed on the pavement. My guts wrench at the sight of her. She looks good, even with her hair covering half her face – pretty and fragile and perfect. I haven't stopped thinking about that day in Brighton, remembering how small she seemed as she talked about Leo, how I wanted to wrap my arms around her and shelter her from any more pain. I wish I could go back to that moment and kiss all her sadness away.

She doesn't smile when she sees me. It's obvious she's drunk but she's a lot more together than I expected, given the way she sounded on the phone. There's no mistaking the anger on her face – I suppose I deserve that. I don't even know what I'm going to say, how I'm going to explain.

Helen doesn't smile either; she just walks towards me. "You've got five minutes."

"Hi, Helen," I say. "Nice to see you again."

Her jaw tightens. "Is it? Is it really?"

"Unexpected," I reply, looking past her to Niamh. "But good all the same."

Now that I'm closer, I can see tear tracks on Niamh's cheeks and I feel a stab of guilt. I did that. I made her cry. As if she doesn't have enough to deal with. "I am sorry, Niamh," I begin.

"You should be," she interrupts. "All you had to do was be honest with me."

Dread washes over me in a freezing tide. What does she mean, be honest? What exactly does she think I've been lying about? "Uh – in what way?"

She stands up then, fury blazing in her eyes. "You should have told me about you and Emily. I'd never have gone out with you if I'd known."

I can't help myself – I let out a shaky laugh of relief because she hasn't figured out my secret. "Me and Emily? What are you talking about?"

Helen points an angry finger at me. "You are a liar and a cheat."

I'll hold my hands up to the liar bit, but a cheat? Where's that coming from?

I stare at Niamh's tight expression and something clicks into place. That's why she thinks I backed off – she's got it into her head that me and Emily are a couple. "You've got it all wrong," I say, sidestepping Helen and walking towards Niamh. "I didn't lie about Emily. She's a friend, nothing more. That's all she's ever been."

She stares at me wordlessly for a minute, evidently trying to work out whether or not she believes me. "Then you lied about fancying me."

Suddenly, I'm reminded that Helen is listening to every word of our conversation. She's not the only one – a station isn't exactly private. But I can't see any alternative – tomorrow, Niamh might not be prepared to listen. The only trouble is, I can't do what she wants. I can't be honest with her. "I didn't lie about that. I…got a bit freaked out about how fast things were moving, that's all."

I hold my breath, waiting to see how she reacts. She glares at me for a moment longer, then sits down heavily on the bench. "You prick."

The air whooshes out of me in relief. "I know," I say, crossing to sit beside her. "Sorry. If you'd answered my messages we could have avoided this."

She shakes her head. "I deleted them."

"So you're not a love-rat," Helen says, her tone withering. "You're just male."

I take Niamh's hand. "In the Marvel comics, there are these two characters, Black Widow and Hawkeye. And sometimes they're on the same team and sometimes they aren't. But they have this chemistry and you know they're meant to be together." Taking a deep breath, I look into her eyes. "That's us. You're Black Widow to my Hawkeye."

Niamh doesn't say anything. There's no anger on her face, just sadness, and I feel even worse. I lift one hand and let it gently brush her cheek. "I'm sorry."

She sighs but doesn't push me away.

"Are you going to remember this happened tomorrow?" I ask. "You're not going to go back to ignoring me, are you?"

"Maybe," she says. "Possibly."

It's not a chance I'm willing to take. Scrabbling around in my pocket, I pull out a half-chewed biro and the screwed-up cigarette packet Marco dropped in the park. I stuff it hurriedly back into my pocket.

"Hold out your hand," I say, and I sketch Hawkeye's bow and arrow on the back. Beside it, I write: *Jonny is very sorry. Please give him another chance.*

She squints down at it. "Did you just draw on me?"

"A bit."

"What if it washes off?"

I tug up the sleeve of her coat and do a more detailed version on the soft flesh of her forearm.

"There, that should last until the morning," I say, covering it back up and pressing her arm gently.

Helen has wandered over to the station doors and is peering at the monitor showing the arrivals and departures. "There's a train in five minutes."

There's a lot more we need to say but it's probably not the time or the place and I couldn't be sure if it was the alcohol or Niamh talking. So I walk them both over to the London-bound platform and wait until the train arrives. Helen climbs aboard straight away and slumps into one of the seats but Niamh hesitates. She opens my jacket, tugs at the T-shirt I'm wearing. It's the skull one she picked out for me in Brighton. And before I can speak, she reaches up and pulls my head towards hers. This time, I don't move away.

NIAMH

Mum slams every door possible on Sunday morning. In fact, I'm fairly sure she slams some of them twice, just to make her point. When I finally surface, around midday, she fires a thin-lipped look of disapproval my way.

"Drinking, Niamh? How could you?"

She's talking really loudly, as though she expects me to have a hangover and is trying to make it worse, except that I dropped a couple of painkillers before I even got up so I'm not feeling too rough. God knows where Dad is – hanging around the Sunday league pitches, probably, trying to pretend Leo is still out there. He'd only take Mum's side if he was here – if he bothered to chip in at all.

I don't remember much from last night, vaguely recall being at the funfair and there's ketchup in my hair, which suggests we had some kind of junk food. Thankfully, my headache is minimal but I could do without another lecture from my mother. Especially one that I know will end with her eyes filling with tears and some kind of reference to Leo. "Can we pretend we had this argument already, Mum? I'm sorry for coming home drunk, okay?"

Even as I say it, I know I've got the tone wrong. She glowers at me and slams her coffee mug down on the kitchen worktop. "No, Niamh, I think it needs saying. We're trying to be understanding and to cut you some slack but..." She sucks in a deep, angry-sounding breath. "Did you stop to think about how dangerous that was? How worried we would be? Anything could have happened."

I dig my nails into my palms, willing myself not to react. "I had a few drinks, that's all. It's hardly abseiling down the Shard."

She shakes her head, ignoring the dig. "Is this a new way of punishing us? Making us worry about whether you've drunk yourself into a ditch, or worse?"

I try to keep a lid on my temper, I really do, but it's like she's deliberately trying to pick a fight. "It's called having a life, Mum. You should try it sometime."

Her lips tighten even further. "There's no need for that."

There's no stopping me now. "Yeah, there is. I'm nearly sixteen years old and you don't seem to get that I can make my own choices."

"Of course I do," she says and there's an undeniable quaver in her voice. "I know you'll find this hard to believe but you haven't always hated me. There was a time when you wouldn't let anyone but me tie your shoelaces, Niamh, and a cuddle could make everything better. And now…"

There's pleading on her face as she trails off, begging me to remember how things used to be. And I don't want to weaken, don't want her to know she's got to me so I harden my heart. "Now I'm big enough to look after myself."

Her expression clangs shut. "That's what Leo thought," she snaps. "I'm just trying to protect you."

"Protect me?" I fire back. "Suffocate me, more like."

The words hang in the silence that follows. She doesn't cry, although I can see her shoulders trembling, and she doesn't shout. She just stares at me for a long wounded second, like she doesn't really know who I am, and then turns away and walks out of the kitchen.

"Mum," I call, already sorry, but she doesn't stop.

I slump against the sink. Now that the anger has evaporated, I'm bruised and weary. I know Mum is struggling, groping her way through a nightmare that won't go away; we all are. And the suffocation comment wasn't a lie – sometimes I really do feel like I can't breathe when she's fussing over me. But it doesn't give me the right to act like a bitch.

I glance over to the fridge door, where a photo of Leo is wedged next to his yellowing match schedule. He's openly grinning, the way he always did when Mum and I argued.

My nails rasp on the thin material of my pyjama top as I dig at the itchy scaly skin on my elbows. Tears prick at my eyes. "Get lost, Leo," I whisper, the way I always did when he was winding me up. "Just…get lost."

Except that I can't help thinking he's not the one who's lost.

We are.

It's not until an hour later, when I pull off my pyjamas to get into the shower, that I notice the smudged bow and arrow on my arm. There were black marks on my hand earlier but I assumed it was just dirt and washed it off. I peer down at my skin, trying to make out the barely legible words beside the picture and then a jumble of images tumble through my head; trains and a station and Jonny. Hurrying back to my room, I pick up my phone and fire off a message to Helen. But even before she replies, I know it's true: we went to St Albans and made Jonny come and meet us. And – a sudden flash of memory – I kissed him again. But this time it was better.

My phone beeps.

6 November 13:16
Hey, Miss Drunk and Disorderly. I think it's safe to say
you and J-boy are speaking again… H x

I climb into the shower and let the water wash the faint
smell of alcohol away. If Jonny and I kissed then we must
have talked about Emily first. Frowning, I chase an elusive
snapshot of Jonny sitting next to me, his face all serious.
I just wish I could remember what he said.

There's a message from Jonny when I get out of the shower.

13:41
How's the head?

I'm not sure how to reply. Clearly, *he* thinks we're back
on friendly terms too but I don't feel any closer to knowing
what's going on in his head. I should probably be honest
and admit I don't remember much of last night.

13:52
Still attached.
Thanks for coming to talk.

13:54

No worries. So are we OK now?

I chew my fingernail. Play it cool or tell the truth?

> **13:59**
> I don't remember much, to be honest.
> Are we?

There's a longer gap between messages this time, so long I check whether mine has actually sent and then get worried I've scared him off with my drunken flakiness. Then the phone rings and his name flashes up on the display.

"Hi," I say.

"I thought I'd better ring, so there are no more misunderstandings," he replies. "Emily is a mate, nothing more. I do fancy you, as I believe I made clear just before you got onto the train. The three blokes who gave us a round of applause definitely thought so. I told you, you're Black Widow to my Hawkeye. And I want to see you again, whenever you're free. Okay?"

Excitement fizzles through my veins. I remember now, that kiss went on and on, right until the guard blew the whistle and the doors started beeping. My lips feel tender, even a little bit bruised and I remember thinking I never wanted it to stop. But seriously, Black Widow to his Hawkeye? So that's what the drawing is about. He's such a comic geek. "Okay," I say, smiling.

"So when do you want to meet up?"

"Now?" I say, only half joking. "I could do with getting out of the house."

There's a pause, then he says, "I wish I could but I've got some stuff to do. I'm around tomorrow, though?"

I wonder if that stuff involves Emily but I don't say it. Instead, I walk downstairs to check the calendar on the back of the kitchen door: three columns, one for each of us and a whole lot of nothing where Leo used to be. "Mum and Dad are out tomorrow afternoon," I say. "Why don't you come round here after school and we'll decide where to go from there?"

This time there's an even longer pause. "Okay," he says slowly, making me wonder what he's thinking. "Where do you live?"

I give him my address. As I hang up, I notice my heart is thudding with anticipation, as though it's excited too. Maybe all his comic-book crap means something after all. Maybe we are meant to be together.

12

JONNY

'm surprised to find Em still tucked away in her own room when I visit on Sunday, instead of back on the ward. One of the nurses hands me a mask and blue latex gloves before he'll let me in to see her, so I know something is up.

"She's immunosuppressed," he says, when I ask if everything is okay. "We're just being careful."

The sight of Em makes my gut clench: she looks bad. Her breathing is laboured and there's a catch at the end of every breath, like she's gasping. There are more bags above her head than ever before, dripping see-through liquids into her veins. Is this why she wanted me to see her – because she's really low?

237

"Em," I say quietly, taking a seat beside her. "What's going on?"

"Stupid chest infection," she says, heaving in another breath. "Can't shake it off. It's even more annoying… because they've said I can go home once my breathing improves."

Her eyes meet mine and I study them for signs that she's lying, that there's something more serious going on. But she doesn't flinch. "You'd tell me if there was anything I needed to know, wouldn't you?"

"Of course I would," she says. "We tell each other everything, right?"

I have to fight not to look away then because I'm scared she'll see right through me and know that I've broken our honesty pact a million times by now. But her expression doesn't change. Instead, she lifts a bony hand to touch her head, which is now covered in a thin layer of fine dark hair. "What do you think?"

"Looking good," I say, adding another lie to the tally.

"And obviously my diet's going well," she adds wryly. Her wrists are so thin I can see the bones through her skin. She coughs, a phlegmy, rasping hack that hurts just to hear it. Once the cough subsides, she dredges up an embarrassed smile. "So that's what's up with me. What's up with you? How's it going on the outside?"

She doesn't have the breath to say much herself, and

the cough means it's easier for me to do the talking. So I tell her about Marco and the others, how I've started to take an interest in football and can even explain the offside rule now. I talk about the guitar my dad gave me and the lessons I'm starting soon. And she seems to approve at first but by the time I finish, she's frowning slightly. "I didn't know you wanted to learn the guitar. You never said."

"There's a lot of stuff I wasn't interested in when I was sick." She's still watching me, staring like I'm a stranger, and I don't want to tell her that some of my new hobbies are things Leo was into too. "You know how it is."

"What about your artwork? You're still doing that, right?" she asks.

The only thing I feel like drawing these days is Niamh, but I keep that to myself. Then again, there's no sign of the picture I drew for Em so she can't be that interested. "I don't really have time for it any more," I tell her.

She lies back on the pillow, her gaze suspicious. An uneasy silence builds.

The awkwardness is almost painful. "I went to the cinema." The words are out of my mouth before I can stop them. "Ate my body weight in crap, all the stuff I'm not supposed to touch."

"Oh? Who with?" she manages and there's a strange look in her eyes.

I hesitate before replying, wondering if I should leave

Niamh out of it. Part of me thinks that I can't tell Em about her now, not after keeping it a secret for so long but on the other hand, I want to. "I went with Niamh. We've...we've been talking a bit. Online..."

I trail off as Em reacts badly. She doesn't look angry, just tight and hurt in a way that makes me feel worse than if she screamed and shouted at me. Is it the fact that I went to the cinema without her that's the problem, or that I went with Niamh?

"I can't wait until you and me can go," I say, speaking fast. "The nachos are going to be on me."

She doesn't speak and I'm horrified to see there are tears in her eyes. I cast around for something to distract her and remember with a flash of inspiration that I've brought her a present: a hairclip shaped like a butterfly I saw on a stall in Covent Garden on my way here. "Here," I say, reaching into my pocket for the package nestling there. "I got you something."

I pull it out of my pocket to give to her and the corner catches on something else. Before I know it, the empty cigarette packet Marco tossed at me earlier in the week tumbles onto the white sheets of Em's bed.

She picks it up and stares at it. "Is this supposed to be a joke?"

I try to laugh but it comes out all dry and weird. "Obviously that's not mine."

Her eyes rest on me and I can see the tears have gone. Instead, she's furious, burning with rage. "Is this a joke, Jonny?"

Reaching out, I try to take the empty box from her but she tightens her grip.

"No," I say. "I told you, it's not mine. Marco dropped it in the park and I picked it up."

"Right. Don't they have bins in the park?"

"Yeah, of course they do. I forgot about it, that's all." I frown, wondering why this is such a big deal. Seriously, I've never seen her so angry. And then it hits me – she thinks I've started smoking. She's lying in hospital, struggling for breath because of a lousy chest infection and she thinks I'm risking my new heart filling my lungs with poison. "Em, I promise you I haven't started smoking. You'd be able to smell it for a start."

Her chest heaves as she glares at me. "I can't believe you'd be so stupid. There are kids in here who'd give anything to have what you have, a chance at life." A coughing fit shudders through her, making me worry it's going to shake her apart but I don't know how to help. A tear rolls down her cheek, then another on the other side. "And what do you do? You throw it all away to impress some losers you've just met."

"Em, calm down."

The tears are flowing fast now and she wipes them

away with bony fingers. "You're not the boy I used to know, Jonny. He would never have been so idiotic, so…so selfish. Someone *died* to give you a heart, or have you forgotten that?"

"Of course I haven't," I say, my ears roaring at the injustice of it all. I wish I'd never bothered to pick the stupid packet up, left it on the ground for that woman to run over with her pram. "I told you it's not mine."

She sucks in a deep, gasping breath. "And now you're chasing this girl, Niamh. Does she know you're not really interested in her, Jonny? That you're using her?"

Her eyes glitter with fury. I stare at her, trying to work out why she's so angry. The cigarettes I get but why does she give a stuff about Niamh? "What are you talking about? We went to the cinema, that's all."

Fresh tears flood down her cheeks. "Liar! I'm not stupid, Jonny, I can see it in your eyes that it's gone further than that."

I'm seriously worried for her now; the machines by her side are starting to beep and her forehead is covered with sweat. And even though I genuinely don't understand why she's going off on one quite this badly, I do know I need to calm her down somehow. "Em, I promise you it's not like that—"

"Get out!" she screams, so loud that the nurse who appears to answer the alarms looks shocked. Em throws the packet feebly at me and it falls to the floor. "Take your lies and your selfishness and...your stinking cigarettes and leave. And don't ever come back."

She subsides into another round of coughing. The nurse doesn't speak, just hurries towards the bed and he doesn't have to say a word to make me feel like crap. Dull heat rises in my cheeks as I stoop to pick up the cigarette packet and walk to the door. Glancing back, I see the nurse check the machines and adjust the drips. Em faces the other way, clearly battling for breath. And though I don't want to go, don't want to leave her like this, it seems like Em is better off without me right now.

6 November 22:47
Niamh. You awake?

           22:48
           Yeah. What's up?

22:50
Can't sleep. I had a row with someone
and now I'm doing that thing where
you think of all the things you should
have said.

22:51

I know exactly what you mean. I used to do
that with Leo all the time. Still do, except
now I win more. Who did you argue with?

22:56

Would you freak out if I told you it was Em?

23:08

Niamh?

23:09

Still here. No, I wouldn't freak out. She's your
mate, you are allowed to talk to her. What
did you argue about?

23:12

Stupid stuff. She thinks I've started smoking.

23:13

HAVE YOU? O.O

23:13

Seriously, you have to ask? I had an empty
cigarette packet in my pocket and she convinced
herself it was mine.

23:15

I can see why she might think that. Is that all it was about?

23:17

Mostly…a bit about you.

23:17

Me? Why?

23:18

She doesn't think I should be seeing you.

23:20

Oh. Why not? Is she jealous?

23:21

No! God, no, nothing like that. It's a bit complicated, tbh, she's got some stuff going on.

23:22

Stuff.

23:22

Right.

23:25

Serious stuff. I'm sure she'll have calmed down
by the next time I see her. You know what girls
are like ;)

> **23:28**
>
> ...er, yeah...

23:30

Anyway, I'd better try to get some sleep. Seeing
a certain someone tomorrow ;)

> **23:31**
>
> OK. Night x

23:33

Thanks for being there, Black Widow. Night x

It takes me for ever to drift off after I say goodnight to
Niamh, especially now I have an extra layer of guilt. I
didn't exactly lie to her but I wasn't completely honest,
either – Em is jealous, just not in the way Niamh thinks.
She's jealous I went to the cinema without her – that
I'm doing our Unbucket list with someone else. Really it
could be anyone and she'd react the same. And it's only

natural that she lost it over the cigarette packet – I'd probably have done the same if I'd been her.

I can't stop replaying the moment the packet fell onto the bed, seeing the look of fury on her face, hearing that wheezy mucus-filled hack as I walked away. Why didn't I bin it? Why didn't I think about how she'd feel if she saw it? The ridiculous thing is, I never got to give her the butterfly clip – it's still in my pocket. I'll go back in a few days, make her see that it was all a misunderstanding, that there's no way I'd be so stupid. One day, we might even look back on what happened and laugh. Maybe.

And then there's the guilty little time bomb of Leo's heart, waiting to go off in our faces and the only way to defuse it is to tell Niamh the truth. That keeps me awake for a long time too – in the end, I grab my sketchbook and draw until my eyes grow heavy. Just before I go to sleep, I fire off a message to Em.

7 November 01:36

I'm sorry I upset you. I'm sorry I'm out here when you're stuck in there. I'm sorry for hurting you, Em. Please don't hate me.

I read it over and over, not sure they're the right words but eventually I hit send. Even if they're wrong, at least it's a start.

* * *

I'm not feeling my best as I make my way to Niamh's house. My head is fuzzy from lack of sleep and I almost missed my medication this morning, that's how messed up I am – Mum had to chase down the street after me, my tablets in her hand. There's a stubborn single tick next to my message to Em, telling me she hasn't seen it yet, which bothers me but not as much as noticing that she's unfriended me on Facebook. She really is furious with me. Even so, I can't wait to see Niamh. I'll just have to pretend I can't hear the quiet tick-tick-ticking of the unseen bomb.

I stand for a minute outside the house, taking in the scene. This is where Leo lived, where he grew up. It's a nice place, bigger than I expected, and in a part of town you need serious money to live in. I don't know what Mr Brody does for a living but whatever it is, it obviously pays well. I try to imagine Leo walking out of the red front door in his football kit, waving to his family as he headed off to a match. Or maybe carrying his guitar, going for a jam session with his band-mates. It's weird thinking that less than four months ago, he was here. Weirder still knowing part of him is back again, inside me.

Niamh answers the door almost before the chime dies away. She stands there in her usual black skinny jeans and a T-shirt, unsmiling as always. "Hi," she says.

"Hi," I reply, wondering if it's too much to kiss her hello but she steps primly back to let me in and my chance disappears.

She takes my coat. "How are you doing? Have you heard from Emily?"

I shake my head. "I messaged her this morning but she hasn't read it. She'll get over it. Eventually."

The glimmer of sympathy in her eyes suggests I sound even less confident than I feel. "Maybe she's blocked you."

I think about that lonely tick. Sent, not delivered. "Nah. She'd never do that."

"Do you want a drink or anything?" she asks, leading me into the living room. "We've got Coke or orange juice if you want."

I lower my rucksack to the floor and take in the scene. There are reminders of Leo everywhere. The mantelpiece is loaded with shiny silver trophies – some big, some small, all Leo's. There isn't a single one that bears Niamh's name. In fact, if I didn't already know Leo had a sister, I'd have no idea from looking at this shelf. There are photographs on a sideboard – some of these feature Niamh at least. The ones from primary school are my favourites – Leo is gap-toothed and grinning the same smile I recognize from Facebook and Niamh has golden bunches on either side of her head, sweeter than her twin, but already less confident. I'm not used to seeing her smiling but there's no mistaking the stubborn angle of her chin. I move from photo to photo, taking it all in, and barely even notice Niamh has gone until she pokes her head back in from the kitchen. "Well?"

"Oh. Water, please," I say, stepping back into the middle of the room. She vanishes again and returns a moment later with a glass. "You should smile more."

The second the words are out of my mouth, I cringe inside. Have I really just told a girl who lost her brother to *smile* more? Jesus, why didn't I go all the way and come out with *Cheer up, it might never happen?*

She throws me a dead-eyed look and hands me the drink. "Have I ever mentioned you sound like my mother?"

"Once or twice," I concede. "But you should. You've got a nice smile."

There's a brief silence, like she's weighing up whether to tell me something, then she shakes her head. "Up until a year ago, I had braces. Full metal ones that made me look like a robot."

I open my mouth to speak but she cuts me off. "Don't even think about comparing me to some bloody comic-book character. Just don't."

And I close my mouth, half pleased, half embarrassed that she knows me so well. "Leo used to tease me about them," Niamh goes on, studying one of the pictures. "He used to say they'd fuse together and I'd have to have all my teeth out or starve to death. I don't know who was the bigger idiot – him for saying it or me for believing him."

My own smile feels suddenly uneasy. On the surface, it sounds like a funny thing to do but I'm getting the feeling Leo wasn't as perfect as I thought he was and it sits uncomfortably with my idea to be more like him. Changing the subject, I wave at the trophies. "Are all these his?"

She pulls a face. "Yeah. There are even more upstairs, his room is full of them. I sometimes used to think he got them for just turning up."

I sip my water, searching again for something that has Niamh's name on it. There's nothing. And I'm starting to understand why she's so conflicted, starting to see Leo as she saw him – a hard act to follow, even now. No wonder she's volatile – you're not supposed to be jealous of the dead. And I realize all over again that there'll never be a good time to tell her about Leo's heart.

"I can't imagine what it's been like for you," I say, even though I sort of can. We saw plenty of grief in the hospital, plenty of families coping, or not coping, with unbearable loss.

Niamh shrugs. "It sucks. Everything falls apart. No one knows what to say so they mumble the same old crap, dumping their own emotions on top of yours. But the worst thing is that everyone thinks they understand how you feel, when they don't have the first clue."

She doesn't sound especially different from normal

but her expression is tight and angry and I can see she's struggling to get a handle on her emotions. I'm no expert but I've seen a few counsellors and I'm pretty sure Niamh hasn't dealt with her brother's death as well as she pretends. There's no way for me to say that without giving myself away, though, so I make a joke. "And telling them to shove it causes offence, right?"

Her mouth twists into a tight-lipped smile. "A bit."

I let out a snort, remembering all the times I wanted to scream at the nurses and doctors to get out, leave me alone. Niamh must see something in my face – a glimmer of understanding, maybe – because she crosses the room and takes my hand. "Come on, I'll give you the tour."

There's more Leo in the kitchen. A photo is stuck on the fridge and when I get nearer, I see there's a football schedule too, pinned by a Chelsea Football Club magnet. Upstairs, Niamh pushes open a closed door.

"Leo's room," she says and I get a confused impression of grunge bands and Chelsea blue from the walls. "He wasn't that tidy. Mum picked up his dirty boxers and hoovers in here once a week. She still changes the bed, believe it or not, like he's going to come home one day."

Her voice is flat, emotionless, but I'm not fooled. "It's okay to miss him," I say carefully.

She glances away, a curtain of hair obscuring her face. "I don't, though."

I know she's lying. It's there in everything she does – she's like a cat curled up around an injury, pretending it doesn't hurt, spitting at anyone who goes near. And I ache for her because I want nothing more than to help, but I don't know if I can: Leo brought us together but he's also standing between us. Or at least, his heart is.

Niamh moves along the landing to a door at the end. When she looks back at me, there's a different look in her eyes, one I'm getting to recognize and it chases all thoughts of her brother from my head. "This is my room. Coming in?"

The invitation thrills me and scares me at the same time. I've never been invited into a girl's room before. Does she want to show me around or does it mean something else? What if she *does* mean something else? No, she can't mean that, it's too soon.

She's watching me, waiting for me to answer. "Can I use the toilet first?" I blurt out, more to buy myself some thinking time than because I actually need to go.

If she has any idea what a tornado she's caused in my head, she doesn't show it. Instead, she points to a door at the end of the hallway, back past Leo's room. "In there. Don't miss."

She goes into her room, leaving me alone. My hands shake as I pee – I have to wipe the bowl when I'm done – and I take as long as I dare washing my hands. The towel is soft beneath my jittery fingers and I force myself to breathe, deep slow breaths, in and out. As I reach for the door, there's a buzz in my pocket – an alarm to remind me to take my pills. I clear the screen, automatically lowering the bag from my shoulder and tugging at the zip. Then I hesitate. If I stop to work out which cocktails of drugs I should be swallowing next, Niamh might think I'm not interested and I'm not chancing that again. I'm starting to hate them, anyway, they're making me fat and I'm sick of having to live by their rules.

Niamh's door is ajar when I leave the bathroom. As I pass Leo's room, I pause in the doorway. This is who he was, the person whose heart is thudding faster than it should in my chest right now. The grunge poster is predictably Nirvana. There are more trophies on a shelf over the bed and an acoustic guitar leaning against the Chelsea bedspread, as though Leo was strumming it right before he left the room. I take a few steps forward, half tempted to pick it up and try the chords I've learned so far but then Niamh would know I'm in here. So I lift up one of the trophies instead and heft it in my hand. *Hampstead Heath Golden Boot*, it says, *Leo Brody*. My heart thumps a tiny bit louder, almost as though it recognizes I'm holding part of its past, a bit of Leo.

I stare down at the trophy, weighing it in one hand like it's gold instead of silver-plated. It's a talisman, something to make me as strong and confident and brave as Leo was – a hero. A winner, maybe even a leader; not perfect but a zillion times better than me. And rationally I know I'll never be as good as that but it doesn't stop me dreaming. I want people to look at me the way they looked at Leo, with admiration, not pity. I want life to be easy, like it was for him. I want his brilliance to become part of me, so I can shine a little bit too.

A noise from next door reminds me I shouldn't be in here. Niamh will be wondering where I am – any second now she'll come looking for me. And if she finds me in Leo's room, she'll want to know what I'm doing and I'll have to tell her the truth; the whole story of who I am.

Maybe that wouldn't be such a bad thing, the voice murmurs. *You're going to have to tell her eventually – why not now?*

In a strange way, it kind of makes sense. I really like Niamh – do I really want to keep something as huge as this a secret from her?

The problem is it will change things; I know it will. And maybe Em's right – maybe I am selfish but it feels like Niamh and me are finally getting somewhere. Now isn't the time to come clean. I will tell her, just not today – not when she's waiting for me next door.

Putting the statue back, I go to find Niamh.

43

NIAMH

Jonny's face is flushed when he walks into my room – he looks almost feverish. I know how he feels. I'm sitting on my bed, my veins fizzling with adrenalin at the sight of him. Mum will wonder why I've tidied up but she'll never guess the truth. I hide a little smile when I imagine her reaction; she'd totally freak out if she knew there'd been a boy here.

"This is my room," I say and immediately want to wince. He knows it's my room, I've already told him that and there's a sign on the door. He doesn't mention my idiocy, though. There's a strange expression on his face as his gaze flickers around, probably noticing that this is the only room in the house with no obvious trace of Leo. He's here if you know where to look: the jumper stuffed beneath my pillow, the stone with the hole I picked up from the beach that I wear as a necklace sometimes, the insulting birthday card he made me last year. And of course I've moved the tablets from under my pillow – they're in the wardrobe for now. But Jonny doesn't look like his mind is on Leo. His eyes are fixed on mine and he's sweating, edgy and excited. "Niamh—"

I stand up, my legs unsteady with my own nervous anticipation, and he stops talking. I hadn't planned to make the first move this time – if he wants me, I decided, he'll have to prove it. But he looks so uneasy that I'm not sure he will. So I step forward and take his hand. "I'm starting to think we're not Black Widow and Hawkeye after all."

He stares down at me and I can see conflict in his eyes, as though he wants me but he doesn't. Then he mutters something I don't catch and his rucksack hits the floor. A second later, he gathers me into a kiss so intense I gasp.

I don't know how long it takes us to tumble onto the bed. I do know that our mouths don't part when we land. It feels incredible to be kissing him again; urgent and hungry but right. Everything tingles, my nerve endings are on fire. One of his hands tangles in my hair, the other lands on my waist.

"Niamh," he murmurs against my cheek. "Oh God, Niamh."

I lie still, marvelling at every new sensation. I feel free, like I'm not really me any more – Niamh Brody doesn't have boys in her room. She definitely doesn't have them moaning her name. And almost the second I realize that, Jonny's mouth stops moving on mine. With a groan that sounds almost like it hurts, he pulls back.

"What's wrong?" I ask, filled with anxiety that I've done something wrong.

He rolls over to lie on my pillow, his eyes closed and his chest heaving. "Nothing's wrong." His forehead creases and he lets out a tiny embarrassed laugh. "I just needed to stop, okay?"

I feel my face go pink. "Oh, sorry."

"Don't apologize," he says, taking a deep breath and sitting up. "It was good. But I – well, I don't want to rush things."

He looks so serious that I want to throw myself on top of him and smother him with more kisses. But I don't. "Get you, being all sensible. You're not exactly a typical teenage boy, are you?"

His glance is sharp at first, then relaxes when he realizes I'm teasing him. "Probably not. But the thing is, I don't really have a clue about any of this. You're – I'm – I haven't done this before."

I really don't think it's possible to like him any more than I do right at that moment. "Me either," I say shyly. "Couldn't you tell?"

"No." He leans over and kisses me again, but this time it's more of a gentle, closed-mouth peck. "As beginnings go, it was pretty good."

"Yeah." I stretch up my hand to stroke his face, brush his lips and chin. My fingertips trail down his throat, over his Adam's apple and slip beneath the neck of his T-shirt. I feel wild and daring as I caress the smooth skin around his collarbone. And then my fingers find something I'm not expecting; the bumps and lumps of puckered skin. A scar.

"What's that?" I say, exploring as far as my fingers will go. I can see the top of it now; a silvery-pink line peeking over the neck of his T-shirt. How far down does it go?

For a moment, Jonny is frozen. Then he pulls my hand away.

I stare at him. "Were you in an accident?"

His face is stricken now, like a deer in the headlights and I don't understand why. "I – it's not what you think."

Now I'm really confused. It's not what I think? "So it wasn't an accident?"

He shuts his eyes. "No," he says quietly. "It was an operation."

I feel myself frown. I don't know much about scars but

I know they fade over time. Whatever the operation was, it wasn't long ago. So why hasn't he mentioned it before now?

"Jonny?" I say, wondering what it is I'm not getting here.

He lies there, eyes closed for a moment, as though he's fighting a battle I don't understand. Long seconds tick by. The silence is heavy, an almost tangible thing between us. Eventually, he lets out a long shuddering breath and looks at me apprehensively.

"There's something I need to tell you."

11

JONNY

I can't stand the way Niamh is looking at me. I'd give anything to rewind the last two minutes, stop her fingers from finding my scar. Now I'll have to tell her everything and I can't breathe when I think about how she's going to react. It feels like I'm about to use petrol to put out an inferno. Christ, I don't even know where to begin.

"I'm listening," she says.

Breathing slowly, I look her square in the eyes. "Before I go on, I want you to know that everything I feel for you is real. You're amazing, Niamh, the best thing that's ever happened to me." Her bewildered expression doesn't change. "I got luckier than I could ever have hoped for when I met you, that's the truth."

She almost laughs. "Get you, Mr Smooth Talker. Look, whatever this is, just get it out. I mean, seriously – how bad can it be?"

It's bad, so much worse than she could possibly imagine. How am I going to do this? "I never wanted to lie to you. Em warned me not to—"

Her expression becomes guarded. "Em? What does this have to do with her?" Then she puts two and two together and comes up with an answer that makes her temper explode like a solar flare. "Oh my God, I *knew* there was something going on between the two of you. That's why you were arguing."

"It's not Emily," I say desperately, running a hand through my hair. "I wish it was that simple."

She calms down a fraction, although her eyes are still molten. "So what is it, then? What have you lied about?"

I roll away from her and sit up. I think I'm about to throw up on her bedroom floor but there's no way I can put this off any longer. I have to come clean. "I should probably have told you this a long time ago."

It all spills out then – how I'd been ill most of my life, how I'd spent most of my childhood in and out of hospital and how close I was to death when a donor heart became available – and I see the exact moment she works it out. All the colour drains out of her face and her eyes fill with horror as I stumble on, trying to explain. Tears stream down her cheeks and she lets out a strangled gasp as she launches herself at me. I don't fight back, don't try to stop the punches from raining down on me because I deserve this and much, much more. I lied to her from the very first moment, when she was already at her most vulnerable, and I heaped lie after lie onto the pile until I can't really remember whether anything I've told her is true.

It isn't until one of her fists lands a crunching blow on the corner of my eye, making me grunt with pain, that she gets a hold of herself and sits back, sobbing and panting, her head in her hands. She hasn't said a word but she doesn't need to.

Helplessly, I watch her cry, overwhelmed with my own misery and regret. I can't believe how badly I've screwed this up. She lifts her tear-stained face to blink at me. "It wasn't me you were interested in at all, was it? It was always Leo, never me."

The pain in her eyes is so sharp it cuts me. "No. That's how it started but believe me, it soon became all about you." I want to take her hand but I haven't got the balls. And then another realization hits me like a freight train. "I really like you, Niamh. I – I – I might even love you."

She stares at me like she's trying to decide whether to believe me and for a second I think I might actually have a chance, that maybe in spite of everything she loves me too. Then she lets out an ugly snort of derision. "Get out," she snarls and her look of venomous hatred makes me flinch. "Get out of my house and never contact me again."

It's no more than I deserve. Even so, there's a lump in my throat as I nod. "For what it's worth, I'm sorry," I croak, standing up and reaching for my bag. "I never meant for this to happen."

She manages a single bark of laughter before turning away. "Go."

My vision goes spotty as I make my way along the landing, forcing me to clutch at the banister as I stumble down the stairs, but it clears when I reach the front door. My phone vibrates as I blunder my way to the main road. It's another reminder to take my medication, I must have hit snooze earlier, but I feel so sick I doubt I'd be able to keep the pills down. All I can see is Niamh's face and the pain I caused – as if she didn't have enough to deal with.

And for the first time since I got Leo's heart, I wish it had gone to someone else.

NIAMH

The only person I tell is Helen. She comes straight over and listens in silent horror as I pour it all out; how Jonny never cared about me at all, how he used me to get information about Leo, how nothing he told me was true. And the worst of it is, as I sit here and recount the whole sorry story, I realize that not only did he take Leo's heart but he took mine too. Except that mine wasn't good enough to hold on to. No, mine he ripped out and trampled into the ground until it was no use to anyone, leaving me an empty hole instead.

"Wow, Niamh," Helen says when I'm done. "I knew there was something off about him, but this? This is seriously messed up."

I slump back on my pillow, scratching at the angry red psoriasis on my elbows and trying not to cry again. "My head hurts."

It's no surprise considering my eyes feel like they've been boiled in salty water and my nose is stuffed with snot. I'm pretty sure my face is a patchwork of swollen blotches but Helen is too good a friend to say so. I don't care anyway – the way I feel right now, I'm never leaving my room again.

"Here," she says, handing me some tablets. "They'll help with the headache."

I swill a few down with water from a bottle by my bed and drop the box onto the bedside table. With a bit of luck she won't ask for them back and I can add them to the emergency supplies under my pillow.

Helen shakes her head. "The only good thing is that you found out what he's like now. Imagine if you'd taken things further…you'd feel a thousand times worse."

She's right, I suppose, but it's not much of a silver lining.

"Just the thought of it is…" She hesitates, not quite meeting my eyes. "It's a bit icky, isn't it?"

I don't get what she means at first. Then I do, and a feeling of revulsion crawls across my skin. "Because Jonny has Leo's heart," I say slowly. "What's your point?"

Now she goes red and shifts around. "Nothing," she

replies, although she sounds a long way from certain. "Forget it. It's not like you're actually related…"

She trails off awkwardly. I shut my eyes, mostly to stop the room swimming. As if I didn't feel bad enough already, now there's this. Turning over, I face the wall and let myself drop into the black pit of my misery. "You should go. I'll text you later."

"Are you sure? I don't think you should be on your own right now. Isn't there anything I can do?"

She sounds nervous and concerned and sympathetic all at once. There's no point in answering her – there's nothing anyone can do, just like there was nothing they could do after Leo died. It's why I stopped going to see Teresa – all those weeks of talking and it never made me feel any better. Jonny didn't really care about me, he used me to get to my brother and the thought that Leo was all he wanted hurts almost more than anything else. And although Helen can't know everything I feel, she does know when to back off.

"Message me later," she says, after a few minutes of excruciating silence.

There's a gentle click from across the room when she leaves, followed by the distant thud of the front door. And another tear squeezes between my tightly closed eyes and trickles onto the already sodden pillow.

* * *

I don't message Helen later. I don't speak to her at all until Wednesday afternoon when she picks her way through the gloom and the clutter of crisp packets and chocolate wrappers covering my bedroom floor to poke me hard in the back. "Why haven't you been at school?"

If it was anyone else, I'd ignore them, the way I ignored my mother when she tried to find out what was wrong yesterday. I blocked her out, counted to a thousand, anything to drown out her entreaties to eat the chicken soup, drink the cup of tea, just talk to her. Dad came and sat on the bed for a while, talked gruffly about how he is always there for me if I need him. That's a joke – he's hardly ever here and I'd have to change my name to Leo before he'd take any interest. But Helen is different; she knows which buttons to push and is almost impossible to ignore.

"I couldn't be bothered," I say, still facing the wall.

I swear I hear her frown. "You can't do this. I know you're miserable but cutting yourself off isn't going to help."

I don't reply.

"Your mum keeps asking me what's wrong," she goes on. "She knows something has happened."

I glance sharply at her then. "What did you tell her?"

Helen looks hurt. "Nothing, of course. Come on, let's go out and do something. Go bowling, catch a film, whatever you like."

"I don't want to go out," I mutter, as I turn back to the wall.

"Then I'll stay here. There's that new comedy show you were on about, remember?"

I do remember. What I remember most is that Jonny and I had planned to watch it in tandem late at night, texting each other little comments as we watched. "No."

She's quiet for a minute. "What can I do to help, Niamh? I'm trying and trying but I don't know how."

The catch in her voice breaks my heart all over again. Helen, my parents – all these people are fussing and crying over me, when I'm really not worth the effort. Things would have been so much better if it had been me who'd died on that beach this summer. They'd have cried then but at least they could have moved on – all I do now is drag everyone else down.

But even Helen's anxious plea isn't enough. "I'm tired. Come back tomorrow."

"How can you be tired?" she answers, and now there's a hint of impatience in her voice, just like my mother gets. "Your mum says you haven't been out of bed since Monday and from the smell in here, I reckon she's right."

This is another Helen tactic – trying to embarrass me into action. I don't know why I feel so exhausted, although I'm not sleeping much at night. Maybe it's the weight of everything that's happened – underneath this mountain of misery there's tiny little me, struggling to hold it all up, and I don't have the energy any more. Jonny's betrayal was the final shovel of crap, the boom that causes the avalanche. And I'm tired of feeling like this too – sometimes I wish I could turn it off. That's where the boxes under my pillow come in; the mother of all off switches.

But I can't explain any of this to Helen; she won't get it. How can she? Perfectly whole Helen, who's never even lost a grandparent. It's easier to close my eyes again and ignore her. Silently, I start to count.

I like numbers, they're steady and predictable. One follows another and there's something soothing in their dependability, comfort in the knowledge that I'll never run out. I don't know how long I count before Helen leaves. Mostly because I don't even notice she's gone.

By Friday, Mum has lost patience with me and stomps into my room with no pretence of sympathy.

"Enough is enough," she says, yanking my bedroom curtains open. The light doesn't work – I took the bulb out on Tuesday. But if she was expecting the room to be flooded with brightness, she must be disappointed – I've taped bin liners across the window to stop the daylight from getting in. It's given me something to focus on, especially when I can't sleep; if I can stop even the tiniest chink of light from getting in, maybe my brain will switch off and I'll feel better. It hasn't worked so far but I'm determined to give it my best shot.

There's a momentary silence when she sees the bin liners. "This can't go on, Niamh," she says, her voice shaking. "You've got to get help."

I suppress the tiniest of smiles then because she has no idea what's lined up underneath my pillow right now. I've gathered quite a collection: Mum's antidepressants plus the other tablets I've picked up over the last few weeks.

"I've been doing some research online," Mum says, sounding much closer, like she's standing next to my bed. She takes a deep breath. "I think you've got post-traumatic stress disorder. We probably all have, to be honest."

The words float over me. Post-traumatic stress disorder; that's the thing soldiers get after being in a war zone or the survivors of a terror attack have for a long time after they walk away from the carnage. Except that I only watched my brother die. Losing a family member is something everyone goes through sooner or later; they don't get PTSD because of it.

"Niamh?" Mum says, sounding desperate. "Please talk to me, sweetheart. Or if you won't talk to me, talk to a doctor. You're scaring me."

She puts her hand on my shoulder then. It's the first time anyone has touched me for days, since Jonny actually.

Her hand feels cool on my sweat-slicked skin but as hard as it is to ignore her, I don't react. Nothing she says can help. No one can. It's easier if they all stay away.

"Niamh," Mum snaps, her voice suddenly sharp with frustration. "For pity's sake, please just talk to me!"

She yanks my arm, pulling it out from under the pillow. The movement is so unexpected that I don't have time to let go of the packet I'm cradling and it flies across the room. It hits the door with a clatter and drops to the floor.

I glance at Mum. She's staring at the box, unmoving. "What is that?" she finally manages, barely louder than a whisper.

She snatches the pills off the floor, reads the label and then holds them up with shaking fingers. "These are mine. What are you doing with them in your bed?"

I take my time answering, trying to sound casual. "Nothing."

"Nothing?" she repeats in disbelief, her eyes resting on my pillow. I do my best to stay calm, willing her to let it go and leave me alone. I don't need her interfering. Then she really loses it, ripping the pillow out from under my head and sending the tablets bouncing – they fly through the air and land at her feet. She stares at them, pale and shaking, then her face crumples as realization dawns. She sinks to the floor, her head in her hands.

"Niamh… Haven't we been through enough?" she sobs.

Dad's feet thunder up the stairs. He stops in the doorway, taking in the scene, and his face turns ashen. "What's going on?"

My mother scoops the boxes off the floor and starts opening them, one after another, checking they're still full. "Look, Ed! Look what she's been hoarding under her pillow."

Dad looks at her hands for a long time, then turns his gaze on me. "Niamh? What's this about?"

I expected him to be furious but his voice is gentle, curious even, and he's looking at me like I'm a favourite toy he's scared is broken. It catches me off guard. "Just... in case. You know..."

He steps over the pills littering the floor to crouch beside my bed. "In case of what?"

"Isn't it obvious?" Mum wails. "She's planning an overdose."

Dad doesn't say anything but the way his eyes flare with pain digs into me like needles under my nails. But worse than that is the flash of understanding that passes between us. The sweat turns cold on my forehead. How can he know what it's like to feel that there's no way back to who you were? Unless he's felt it too...

My head fills with roaring. Dad is the strongest of us; battered, wounded but still the one holding Mum and me up. If he's faltering, what hope is there for us?

My hands tighten on the duvet as I stare at him, wanting to be wrong. "But you're fine," I say to him. "I hear Mum crying in the night, but you…? You're coping."

His expression freezes. "You hear that?"

Mum stares at him, confusion written all over her glistening face. "Hear what? I don't cry at night. Not any more."

"Don't pretend, Mum," I say, pressing the heels of my hands into my eyes. "I know you creep into Leo's room when you think we're asleep. You're not as quiet as you think."

"But I don't go in Leo's room," Mum says, shaking her head. "I can't."

What is she talking about? Of course she goes in there – how else is it the cleanest room in the whole house? Yet there's no sign of deceit in her expression – she seems honestly mystified. But if it isn't her crying in the night—

Dad doesn't meet my questioning gaze. "I didn't realize anyone could hear," he whispers. "Sorry."

Now Mum has worked it out. Her eyes fill up as she looks at Dad. "You, Ed?"

Things are starting to tumble into place now. The long hours he's been putting in at work, the way he can't look at me sometimes, his reluctance to get rid of anything belonging to Leo: I assumed they were signs he was dealing with Leo's death in his own way. I thought Mum was

274

the one struggling to hold it together when all the time it was Dad. *He* tidies Leo's room and changes the sheets. He hides in the dark of the past and he keeps all his sadness concealed.

"Why pretend you're okay?" I say, digging my nails into my palms to stop myself from crying.

"I have to," Dad says quietly. "I have to pretend every day that he's just gone away for a little while, that he'll be back any minute. I can't get used to the fact that he's gone so I persuade myself he hasn't. Every morning, I tell myself the same lie but it wears off in the night."

Mum is staring at Dad like he's someone she's never seen before. "But…you never said…"

"How could I?" Dad asks, spreading his hands. "You need me to be strong. What use am I if I fall apart?"

"Oh, Ed," Mum croaks. "You don't need to hold me up. I'm okay."

He shakes his head. "You're not, Grace," he says, and his eyes fix on mine. "None of us are."

He's right. We haven't been okay since Leo died. It doesn't help that I'm a living, breathing reminder of Leo – a punch in the stomach every time either of them looks at me. But there's more to it than that. It's the thing we all know deep down but no one wants to admit: Dad wishes I'd died instead of Leo. They both do. And the truth is, I wish I had too.

He holds out his arms and Mum stumbles into them. An arrow of guilt pierces me as I watch. It's my fault they are crying now.

"I'm sorry," I mumble, hanging my head so I can't see them any more. "I'm so sorry…"

"Sorry for what?" Dad asks, sitting on the edge of my bed. "The tablets? I don't think you ever would have used them."

I don't answer, avoid his eyes.

"Niamh?" he says, taking one of my clammy hands in his. "What could you possibly have to be sorry for?"

All I have to do is close my eyes to shut them out. But there's a flicker of something at the back of my mind, a memory of Jonny telling me how guilty he felt that he was only alive because Leo had died. And I know I have a choice to make: lie to my parents again or admit the truth, the thing I've been hiding from ever since that day on the beach. I draw in a ragged breath. "I'm sorry we climbed the rocks. I'm sorry I let him fall." I look at them both and a wave of agony surges through me. "I'm sorry I didn't die instead of Leo."

Mum lets out a gasp. Dad's eyes swim with tears. "Oh, Niamh."

And I don't know if it's saying the words aloud or the bear hug my father wraps me in but something seems to break inside me and I cry like I've never cried before.

All the anguish and shock at watching Leo die, all the guilt of knowing it was my fault he was on the rocks in the first place, all my resentment at being left behind – the one who lived; it all washes out in a tidal wave of heartbreak and my parents do their best to weather the storm but they're on the edge of the abyss too. Dad smoothes my hair, listening with silent tears of his own. Mum holds on to both of us, her face a mess of mascara and misery. And eventually, in among all the sorrow and regret and the emptiness, something changes. Not much but enough to leave me feeling peaceful in a way I haven't done for months. Suddenly, I can barely keep my eyes open. I don't protest when my parents lower me to the pillow, nor do I stir when they pick up the boxes from the floor and take them wordlessly away. I sense them pause in the doorway.

"It wasn't your fault, Niamh," I hear my dad say. "It wasn't anyone's."

46

JONNY

The first clue I have that my parents are ill is when Mum refuses to bring my medication into my room on Monday morning.

"It's just a cold," she calls through the door, sounding so bunged up I can barely understand her. "But I'll leave your tray out here. Better to be safe than sorry."

I still have to be careful about infections, but getting a cold isn't as risky as it was three months ago. Even so, Mum's not taking any chances, to the point that she won't even be in the same room as me. Dad lets me walk to college so that I don't have to sit in the car "with his germs" and when I get home, I discover he left work at lunchtime, which never happens. By Tuesday morning, they're both burning up and I ignore their objections and take the day off from college.

"Ask Aunty Rose to come over," Mum says, when I take them up a Lemsip each. "You shouldn't be in here. What if you get ill too?"

I smile, plumping her pillows and handing her a honey and lemon drink. All the years she looked after me and she can't let me do the same for her. Besides, Aunty Rose is a teacher: she can't come over during the day. "Don't worry about me, Mum. Concentrate on getting better."

Dad is sleeping beside her, his mouth wide open, snoring because his nose is blocked. He looks hot, even though the window is open and it's sub-zero outside.

"You're taking your medicine, aren't you?" Mum asks, her eyes following as I place Dad's drink on his side of the bed. "You are writing them down on the sheet?"

I'm grateful that she can't see too clearly in the half-lit room. There've been times I've forgotten a dose, here and there, but lately I've skipped them by choice. "Yes, Mum, of course I am."

She nods, lying back on the pillow. "Good," she murmurs. "Good lad."

When I go downstairs, I scrabble through my college bag for a pen and set about copying her carefully recorded doses from the week before. There are pages and pages of sheets, going right back to the very first day I came home from hospital, almost three months ago. Once I've filled in two days of missed doses, I check my pill box, taking out the ones I've missed and putting them in a small brown bottle that's stashed under the pillow in my room. I can't see the point of taking twelve different medicines that don't make me feel any different. What Mum doesn't know won't hurt her. And physically I've never felt better – it's my head that's messed up now, not my body.

It's actually good to be making my own choices. Snapping open a can of forbidden Coke, I settle in front of the TV, idly doodling in the margins of the medicine sheets. My phone flashes up a message. A tiny hope flares that it might be from Niamh but of course it's not: I'm surprised to see Em's name instead. She's ignored every message I've sent her – I assumed she'd blocked me, to be honest, but apparently not.

15 November 09:26

Hi Jonny. Sorry for losing it last time you came – new medication made me a bit psycho. I'm not allowed visitors, but they're talking about letting me leave soon. Anyway, I just wanted you to know I'm not angry any more. Love, Emily xx

I almost laugh, because I've seen Em react badly to her

medication before and psycho is not the word. Shaking my head with a smile, I tap out a reply.

> 09:37
> Hey Chemo-Girl. FINALLY. Has anyone ever told you you're bloody scary when you're angry? No wonder your cancer surrendered ;)

It takes a while for her to reply, and even then it's only two little words.

> 10:22
> Ha ha.

I'm guessing the new meds also make her sleepy – sometimes the doctors struggle to fine-tune the dosage. But I'm glad she's got in touch and even more pleased she's not angry any more – maybe I haven't lost everything after all.

> 10:24
> So does this mean we can be Facebook friends again?

She doesn't reply to that.

NIAMH

I've never sat in the memorial garden at school. Before Leo died, I hardly even registered it was there – just somewhere we cut through on our way to the English block. But the family counsellor Teresa recommended has encouraged us to face up to the fact that Leo is gone and part of that involves going to the cemetery or, for me, here. Which is why I am spending my first lunch break back at school under an umbrella, contemplating a stone footballer taking a free kick he'll never see through.

It's been an emotional five days. We spent Saturday and Sunday just talking, spilling our guts about everything, which is probably one of the hardest, most exhausting things I've ever done. We agreed we wouldn't lie any more, wouldn't hide from how we felt. I'm careful to keep the Jonny stuff general – I don't think anyone is ready for that little grenade – but skating around something isn't lying, no matter what Helen says. I had an emergency appointment to see Teresa on Monday and talking to her seems easier now that I've stopped treating it like some kind of game I have to win. I'm hoping the family counselling will help too – once we get past the weirdness.

So now I'm sat here on a wet Wednesday lunchtime, nervously gnawing on a fingernail, waiting for Helen to show up. I came in late this morning so I haven't seen her yet but I wouldn't really blame her for ignoring the text I sent her last night, asking her to meet me here. Especially since it's raining.

I'm about to give up and leave when she appears in the doorway opposite. She stands there for a second, staring at me and my dripping umbrella. Then she opens her own umbrella and picks her way through the puddles to perch on the bench beside me. "You picked a great day to come back."

"I didn't get much choice," I say. "It's been pouring all week, anyway."

"Could be worse," she says, after a moment. "It could be raining sharks."

I glance at her cautiously, wondering if the reference to our favourite bad movie means what I hope it means.

There's a wry twist at the corner of her mouth – another clue that maybe she's forgiven me. "True," I acknowledge, and take a deep breath. "So what's new?"

"Not much," she says, pulling a face. "But then it's only been a week since our argument."

I frown at her – a week is a lifetime between best mates. "Surely you've got some tiny morsel of gossip to offer me?"

She shakes her head. "Nope. My mother has decided I need to start yoga, to counteract the impending exam stress. How about you?"

Where to start? I wonder and puff out my cheeks. "I'm jumping off a building next month. You can sponsor me if you like."

She raises her eyebrows. "Family suicide pact? Good plan."

I can't decide whether to laugh: Helen doesn't know about the tablets yet and I'm not sure I'm ready to tell her. I will eventually, once I've got my head around it all. The counselling is helping with that too – we're closer to being a family now, an imperfect, scarred one but nearer than we've been for a long time.

I read this article online once about how people who are drowning don't look like they are – they don't wave their arms around and splash, they don't cry out or scream, because they're too busy trying to breathe. Even the strong can drown; quietly, without fuss, while everyone else thinks they're fine. And now I know that's what was happening to me; I was using all my energy just to keep my head above the water, unable to spare the breath to ask for help. I wasn't coming to terms with Leo's death, coping the way I thought I was. I was drowning in his loss. We all were.

So when Mum does her charity abseil down the Shard in January, Dad and I will be doing it too, along with Sophie, who I'm learning to tolerate, if not like. "The opposite, I think. It's supposed to be life-affirming, or so our new counsellor says."

"Sounds it," Helen says. "You're seeing a new counsellor?"

"Yeah. As a family."

She pulls a face. "Ah. How is it going?"

"It's taking a bit of getting used to," I admit. "We're not allowed to lie."

Helen looks interested. "How would anyone know? Do they hook you up to a lie-detector?"

"Not exactly."

I'm not actually sure how to explain it – I could lie but I don't really want to, it feels like cheating somehow. I wish I knew our counsellor's secret – I could bottle it and make a fortune.

The silence stretches again, filled by the relentless pitter-patter of rain on our umbrellas. I didn't drag Helen out here in a downpour so we could discuss my family's therapy. I'm supposed to be building a bridge back to normality, which sounds like the biggest load of psychobabble ever except – *except* – for the first time in years, I want to feel normal. Not angry, not resentful, not alone, not lost, just normal. And to do that, I need to make up with Helen. "I'm sorry," I say quickly. "I was a cow to you and it wasn't fair."

"Yes," she replies, her gaze fixed on Leo's statue. "But you had a good excuse."

I hesitate, not sure if she means Leo or Jonny or both.

"Have you heard from him?" she asks.

I guess she means Jonny. I hope she does, anyway. "No."

She throws me a curious look. "How are you feeling about him now?"

"Okay," I say slowly, because of all the things I've talked through in my one-to-one sessions, Jonny has been the subject I feel least sorted about. "Not bad. I think I'm over him."

"Good." She nods. "That's good. It would never have worked out, you know that?"

"Yeah," I say, trying not to sound wistful. I don't want to miss Jonny, but there's part of me that does. I have to remind myself every day that he lied to me about everything – I'll never know how much of what he said and did was real and how much was just a way of getting more information about Leo.

Teresa says ultimately very little of Jonny's actions were about me. She didn't mean that in an insulting way, or that he wasn't interested in me at all, more that his bad behaviour was to do with his own issues. Getting a new heart after being ill for so many years must be kind of a big deal; I can see it would take some getting used to. That doesn't mean what he did was right. But I sort of understand more now.

I can't admit any of that to Helen, though. The jury is back, and as far as she's concerned, Jonny has no redeeming qualities, no defence at all. And on the basis of the evidence we have, I don't really feel I can argue.

48

JONNY

On Saturday morning, Mum's sister, Rose, comes over again and practically pushes me out of the house.

"Go and get some fresh air," she insists, when I try to protest. "You look like death warmed up."

I'm not surprised – I haven't left the house much since Tuesday. I've done a lot of sketching, though; it feels good to have a pencil and paper in my hands again. It helps to keep my mind busy, I've found.

I think about getting on a train, going to stand outside Niamh's house but that's nothing new – I've thought about doing that every day for the last week or so, ever since the moment she kicked me out of her life. And then I think about going to see Em but she hasn't given me the all-clear to visit again yet. I'm looking forward to a decent bit of banter when I do.

I wander aimlessly for a while and then I remember the lads have a kick-about in the park on Saturdays. Marco's been nagging me to join them for weeks. When he spots me walking across the frost-covered grass, the first thing he asks is if I'm okay.

"Jackson was hoping you were dead," he says, jogging over from where the others are standing around talking.

"Sorry to disappoint him," I say, glancing over to see Jackson and Eavis glaring at me. "I'm alive and well. My parents were ill so I had to do a tour of duty with them." I roll my eyes in a "What can you do?" way.

Marco grins. "Listen," he says. "I've been meaning to ask you how things turned out with that girl. Did you find the guts to go for it or what?"

I blink and look away. "We broke up."

Marco looks genuinely mortified. "Sorry, man. I would never have said anything if I'd known."

"Why do you care?" I ask, folding my arms defensively. What if he's fishing for ammo to spread around the others?

But he surprises me. "Because you really liked her," he says, throwing me a sideways glance. "And because we're mates. I look out for my mates."

He holds my gaze for a minute, just long enough to convince me he's not taking the mick, then jerks his thumb towards the others. "So, fancy a game? We're a player short."

It's a cold morning, our breath puffs in the frosty air but even so, I'm hot and a little shivery: I must be coming down with my parents' cold. I think about going home, grabbing one of their Lemsips and going back to bed, except that I'm out now and the lads are a player short. Who knows, some fresh air and exercise might be exactly what I need to chase the germs away.

I peel off my coat, then remember the dig Jackson made about my weight last week, when he asked if I inflated myself with a foot pump every morning. It stung and I don't want to set myself up for any more. "Okay. I'm not going in goal, though."

Marco shrugs. "Charlie, you're in goal."

The others look up as we approach. Most of them I know already – Charlie, Billy, Jackson and Eavis from college – but there are a few unfamiliar faces. Marco introduces them and I nod a greeting. Jackson smiles unpleasantly at me. I count silently to ten, awaiting the inevitable low-rent threat and sure enough, he doesn't disappoint. "You're going down, fat boy."

I raise a cool unruffled eyebrow. "Is that what Mrs Walsh says when you dream about her?"

Charlie guffaws loudly and everyone else is right behind him. Jackson's neck turns an ugly shade of deep red as he kicks the ball away. He doesn't answer back, though, and I reckon I've got some filthy tackles heading my way.

Even with ten of us, the game is hard work. There's a lot of running, a lot of tracking back and defending. At first, I'm all right; my fitness has improved a lot since I started joining in the kick-abouts, but fifteen minutes in, I notice I'm more breathless than I should be. I'm sweating too, I can feel it running down my back and cooling on my clothes. I slow down as a sudden cough catches me by surprise and rest my hands on my knees.

"Jonny, man on!"

I look up to find the ball is whizzing through the air towards me. At the same time, I see Jackson bearing down on me, a sneer of utter hatred on his face. Forcing myself upright, I bring the ball down and dance out of Jackson's way, sprinting towards the goal. There's a dull ache in my chest as I run but I can see a way through the defenders, the exact place to put the ball where the goalie won't be able to reach it, and I ignore the pain and weave my way through. Glancing up one final time, I pull back my foot and hit the ball sweetly in the centre. I watch as it soars towards the goal and hold my breath. If it hits the back of the net, I'll feel like Leo's heart finally fits me.

The goalkeeper lunges and misses. The ball shakes the net. And my four teammates pile on top of me, roaring like we've just won the World Cup.

The pain hits me so hard I can't breathe. For a second, I think it's their weight bearing down on me, crushing me into the freezing ground. But then they get up and the pain doesn't go away. If anything, it gets worse. I try to suck in some precious oxygen but my lungs have started to spasm and I cough instead. Tiny pinpricks of darkness dance before my eyes and my head feels like a helium balloon that's coming loose from my body. There's a weird wheezing noise that sounds like a broken-down steam train but is actually coming from inside me. Dimly, I'm aware of voices, shouting, but they're so very far away. I should try to get back to them but even now, I can feel my grip on consciousness slipping. Shadows cluster at the edge of my vision. I slip into their waiting arms and everything goes black.

The first thing I see when I wake up are the squares. Big white squares floating over my head like really unimaginative cubist clouds that come in and out of focus when I blink. I've seen these squares before, I think blearily. I've seen them a lot.

"You're awake," a voice says. "Welcome back."

It takes a lot of effort to move my head far enough to find the owner of the voice – I'm tired, creaking, and my muscles are slow to respond. When I do, I see a familiar face: Mr Bartosinski. He's standing at the bottom of the metal-framed bed, a clipboard in his hand. So that's why the squares are so familiar – I'm back in hospital.

I frown, or try to but even that takes effort. I feel like I've run the Great Wall of China. "What's going on?" I manage.

Mr Bartosinski doesn't smile. "You've had some complications with your heart. It was touch and go for a while but we think we've reversed the rejection and you're on the mend."

What he's telling me doesn't make sense. I was fine, everything was going great – the numbers were good. Why would my immune system reject my heart after ignoring it for months? I stare at Mr Bartosinski in bewilderment.

"You stopped taking your medication," he says gently, without a trace of accusation or anger. "Without the right levels of immunosuppressants, your body attacked your heart. Thankfully, the damage was minimal and heart function has been restored – because I don't imagine you'd get another chance."

He means another heart – I'd never get another heart that matched as perfectly as Leo's. It's a miracle I even got his. Shame floods through me as I remember; I did stop taking some of the pills. I'd decided I didn't need them. "But I felt okay…"

Mr Bartosinski nods. "You would, for a short time."

There's a hint of resignation about his smile. "You're not the first organ recipient to stop taking the drugs and you won't be the last. Teenagers in particular seem to struggle with the demands of life after transplant, especially once they start to feel better – you think you're invincible and can manage without your medication."

An image of Iron Man flashes into my mind and I push it guiltily away. It doesn't make me feel any better that I'm not the first person to ignore the doctors. People die waiting for a new heart and here I am tossing mine aside.

"Unfortunately, it's an illusion," he goes on. "Your good health depends on your prescribed drugs and without them you become ill very fast indeed, as you have discovered."

His words make me feel two centimetres tall. Another thought hits me – my parents. After years of fear and uncertainty, they must have thought they were through the worst of it. Then this happens and suddenly they're almost back where they started. They must hate me.

Mr Bartosinski notices my anxious, darting gaze. "Your parents were here almost constantly while your condition was serious but once you started to respond to the medication, they relaxed a little. I believe they went for breakfast a little while ago."

Relief washes through me like a monsoon. I owe them an apology – a big one. "How long have I been in here?"

"Forty-eight hours. We gave you several concentrated doses of drugs to stop the rejection taking hold so you might not remember much of the last two days. They have some fairly potent side effects too, hence the fatigue and flu-like feeling."

Actually, that's a good description – it does feel like I have the flu. But he's right, I don't remember anything about coming to hospital. My last memory is playing football in the park. From then on, it's all blank. I don't know how I came to be here. I can imagine, though. A sudden lump appears in my throat and I have to look away. I'm not sure I even deserve this second chance.

Mr Bartosinski jots a few things down on my notes and clips them back onto the end of the bed. "Don't beat yourself up too much. The most difficult part of any kind of organ transplant is learning to live with it afterwards. We do what we can to help but ultimately it's up to you to look after yourself." He throws me a sympathetic look. "Try to get some rest."

I lie staring up at the ceiling for a long time after he's gone, listening to the sounds outside my room. I'd forgotten how noisy hospitals are, the constant clatter and chatter. Only the high-dependency and intensive care wards are quiet, and this is the cardiac ward, humming with everyday tasks and conversations. I used to drown it out but now it grates on my nerves, making me ever more on edge as I contemplate how badly I've screwed up – first with Em, then with Niamh and now with this, my supposed fresh start. At least, the medical staff can fix my heart. It's a shame they can't sort out the rest of me.

NIAMH

Helen is uncharacteristically quiet on Wednesday morning. She won't tell me what's wrong, looks away when I try to make eye contact. It isn't until lunchtime and we're sitting outside the science block that she gives in to my persistent questions and lets out an enormous sigh. "I know I'm going to regret this but I suppose you need to know…"

"What?" I say, frowning. "What do I need to know?"

She fiddles with the zip on her coat, clearly reluctant to say, and just as I'm about to reach over and shake her, she sighs again. "Okay. Just hypothetically, what would you do if you knew Jonny was in hospital?"

Now it's my turn to stare. "What do you mean,

hypothetically?" I say, stomach lurching. "Has something happened with his heart?"

Leo's heart.

"Yeah, I think so," Helen says. "I've been keeping an eye on his Facebook, just in case he started bitching about you."

"And?" I demand.

She shrugs. "He hasn't even mentioned you actually."

"Not that, you numpty," I practically howl, thinking of all the articles about transplants I've read since I found out the truth. "Why is Jonny back in hospital? Is he okay?"

"I don't know," she admits. "There are some 'get well soon' messages on Facebook, people talking about going to visit him. He hasn't replied to any of them so I wondered perhaps if—"

I don't let her finish the sentence. "Show me," I say, pointing to her phone.

She hands it over, her expression half amused, half resigned. "You told me a lie, Niamh Brody."

I'm not really listening, too busy looking for clues that he's okay. The "get-well"s start five days ago, on Saturday. "Mmm?"

"You lied to me when you said you were over him," Helen says, watching me. "You're not over him. You're not even close to being over him."

At last, I find a name I recognize and start scrolling

through the messages he's left. I'd love to argue with Helen, tell her she's wrong – I'm concerned about Leo's heart, that's all. I want to know for my parents' sake that it's still beating. But deep down, I know she's right.

And I don't know quite what to do about that.

I stand outside the hospital for the longest time, just before evening visiting hours start, steeling myself to go in. It's not that I don't want to see Jonny – okay, part of it is that I don't want to see him, but mostly it's because I haven't got a clue what to say to him. I still don't know who he is. But I've tried my hardest to stop thinking about him and I can't: I need to see him. No matter how much he hurt me, I need to make sure he's okay. And besides, if having Leo for a brother taught me anything, it's that love isn't a tap you turn off when you don't want to care any more. It seeps into your soul, wears a path to your heart and leaves an unbearable emptiness when it's gone. And I do love Jonny.

So here I am, about to give him one last chance. If he wants it.

His face is a picture when I stop a few metres from his bed. He's not alone – a man and a woman are with him;

his parents, I guess. They turn round when Jonny's eyes widen and I almost run for the door I've just walked through.

"Niamh!" he says, his voice a mixture of surprise and pleasure. "I – how…?"

He lapses into silence, staring at me as though I'm a mirage in the desert. And although it's a shock to actually see him in hospital, he looks better than I expected. In fact, apart from the puffiness around his face, he looks just like the Jonny I knew. Or thought I did.

I take a step forward. "Hi."

His parents are watching me but there's no sign that they recognize my name, which I hope means he hasn't told them about discovering his donor's identity. Now that I'm nearer, I can see traces of Jonny in both of them; he gets his grey eyes with those mesmeric touches of gold from his father and the long eyelashes and full mouth come from his mum. They're both tall and slim, which doesn't surprise me; I read up on heart transplants and discovered patients often put on weight in the first year because of all the drugs they take. That also explains the soft downy hair on the back of his neck when I kissed him – steroids make you hairier, apparently. None of that ever bothered me anyway – it was all about who Jonny was inside. That's what I fell in love with. But it's amazing how many things dropped into place once I knew about his heart.

Jonny's mother steps forward, her eyes bright and inquisitive. "Lovely to meet you, Niamh," she says, holding out a hand and looking me discreetly up and down. "I don't know, you wait for ages to meet Jonny's friends and then two come along in one week."

Behind her, I see Jonny start to go red and a look of mutual understanding flashes between us. *Parents*, it says. *Never knowingly unembarrassing.* I take the offered hand and shake it, repeating the process with his dad. Then there's an awkward silence while we all look at each other until Jonny's mum clears her throat and glances meaningfully round. "We were just going to get a coffee, weren't we, Steve?"

Jonny's dad frowns. "Were we?"

"Yes," his mum says brightly. "So we'll leave you two to catch up."

She beams at me and I see Jonny has her smile too. Then they're gone and it's just us. Another awkward silence hangs in the air. "How did you know?" Jonny asks eventually. "That I was here, I mean."

He waves at one of the chairs by the bed and I sit, trying not to stare at the drips and wires hanging off him. "Helen looked you up online, saw a load of get-well messages." I look at him then. "So I asked Marco what was going on."

Jonny groans. "Oh God, what did he say to you? Was he an idiot?"

A small smile crosses my face. "No, he was all right actually. He seemed genuinely concerned about you. Has he been to visit?"

"Yeah," he says. "He's the other friend my mum mentioned. She almost fainted when she saw him but he won her over, especially when she found out he was the one who called the ambulance."

No visit from Emily, then. "You must have more than two friends."

His expression brightens. "It turns out I do, actually. Quite a few kids from college have come, in between my parents' visits. Even Jackson came and he hates me." He studies me, the tiniest of frowns creasing his forehead. "I'm amazed you bothered, to be honest. I'm even more amazed Helen let you."

I shrug. "She thinks it'll give me closure."

His expression changes the moment I say it. "Closure," he echoes softly. "Right."

I could leave it there if I wanted to – make some small talk and then walk away, having satisfied myself that he's okay. He has no expectations, no hope that I want anything more than an apology and a proper goodbye, one that doesn't involve me screaming at him. And if I'm honest, I wasn't one hundred per cent sure what I wanted until I saw him. But now I am.

I meet his gaze steadily. "Why, Jonny? People have

organ transplants every day and most of them respect the need for anonymity. Why did you need to know about Leo so badly?"

His eyes close briefly and he lets out a long sigh. "It's a bit complicated. I'm not even sure I understand myself."

I wait for him to go on, watching him pull together the nerve to try to explain. Whatever he says will affect my next move – the least I can do is give him the time to get it right.

"I think I wanted to be him," he says simply, looking me directly in the eyes. "I'd been ill for so long I had no idea who I really was and…and I was scared to find out that I wasn't worth a second chance at living. So I hid behind Leo."

I feel my face go slack – whatever I was expecting, it wasn't this.

"I've never been able to do much," he goes on. "I never played sport or joined in with the playground games like all the other kids. I didn't have many friends, as my mother so kindly pointed out. Being ill makes you different." He shakes his head. "And I was never bright enough, never popular enough to get over that.

"Once I was hospitalized, it didn't matter so much, partly because I was so ill but partly because hospital kids get where you're coming from. For the first time in pretty much for ever, I made friends." He stops and offers me a lopsided smile. "That's where I met Em."

Now that he's said it, I remember seeing some photos of her in hospital the first time she messaged me. The thought makes me feel physically sick. All the times I've been jealous of Emily, all the times I've wanted to stick pins into a doll of her and wished she didn't exist…when she was his mate from their time in hospital? Oh my God, I might seriously throw up from the guilt.

"I'd almost given up hope when they told me there was a heart. And then afterwards, I couldn't stop thinking about the donor – the person who'd died and given me my life back. I knew it was someone young, a boy around my age. But no matter how many times I told myself that it didn't matter who the heart had belonged to before, it still ate away at me until I had to do something. And once I'd found him, I wanted to know everything." He lies back on the pillow, his eyes searching my face. "Which is where you came in."

It's almost too much to process. My mouth is dry – I take a nervous swig from my bottle of water. "What's wrong with Emily?"

Some of his tension melts away. "Acute myeloid leukaemia," he says. "One of the worst kinds there is but she's beating it."

He looks proud when he says it and a fleeting spasm of jealousy whips through me before I push it away. I refuse to be envious of a girl who has cancer, even if it turns out Jonny *is* really in love with her instead of me. "Is she still here?"

"They're keeping her in isolation at the moment, something to do with a new drug. She says they're letting her go home soon, though," he replies, and he smiles. "You'd like her, I think."

I breathe a silent sigh of relief. It doesn't matter how nice she is, I don't think I could handle meeting her right now. "I'm sure I would."

"So, that's it," he says. "The whole fugly story. Basically, I was a sponge, trying to suck up Leo's coolness. Except that all I managed to do was hurt you and I'm really, really sorry for that."

He looks genuinely remorseful, I think. His grey eyes, the ones that remind me of storm clouds with the sun piercing through, are serious and sad. "So who are you?" I ask, almost fearful of his answer. "Who are you really, when you're not trying to be Leo?"

Jonny watches me in silence for a minute, then points to a cupboard next to the bed. "In there."

I get up and walk slowly towards the cupboard, wondering what I'm going to find. If it's a Chelsea kit, I'm walking out. But it isn't anything like that. It's a sketchbook. I glance at him questioningly. "Open it," he says, closing his eyes. "That's the real me."

I flick open the cover and it's all I can do not to gasp,

because the picture on the first page is incredible. It's a manga-style drawing of a girl with a mane of electric-blue hair and enormous shining eyes. She has dimples in each cheek and a cute little smile. And she's kicking a giant pink blob monster in what I imagine are its nuts. But it's not the subject matter that makes me gasp – it's the skill of the artist. Greedily, I turn to the next page, and the next; each picture is better than the one before. They're not all manga – some are pencil drawings, others are pastels. The subject matter varies dramatically, from people to animals, trees to buildings, peachy-pink sunrises to gorgeous yellow and red sunsets. The girl with the blue hair crops up a lot in different poses. *Emily*, I think to myself, knowing I'm right. *That's Emily*. And something cracks a little inside me when I see how often he's drawn her. He must love her if he recreates her this often. What do artists call someone who inspires them – a muse?

I'm so absorbed in the book that I almost forget where I am. And then I reach the last page and I'm suddenly, acutely, back in the here and now. Because the last page isn't one drawing, it's loads. He's drawn the same face over and over, like summer roses running riot across a garden wall. At the heart of the page, there's one master portrait, exquisitely done in bold pencil strokes and feather-light shading. The detail is breathtaking, the face is alive. It's a thing of incredible beauty.

It's also – me.

Uncertainty rushes over me. I don't have the presence of mind to count them but I reckon there are more than thirty drawings of me. If the pictures of Emily suggested Jonny was in love with her, what does this mean for me?

"Now that you're here, I'm not sure I've got your nose right," Jonny says, his voice dry. I hear the nerves vibrating beneath the words – he's worried I'll hate it. I don't hate it. I love it. I love *him*.

"They're amazing," I say huskily, blinking hard to dissolve the tears that are threatening me. "You're amazing. What the hell were you doing trying to be Leo when you could do this? He would have killed for talent like yours."

He shrugs. "It felt a bit lame, like something I only did because I was too sick to do anything else."

I look down at the book again and the sight of myself repeated over and over makes me dizzy, so I flick back through the pages. "These are amazing," I repeat. "And I'm not just saying that because some of them are me."

There's the briefest of pauses before he says, "You fill my head, you know."

I glance up sharply, the breath catching in my throat. "What?"

His cheeks turn pink but he doesn't look away. "Right from that first time I saw you, at the fundraiser, you filled my head. I haven't been able to draw anything but you since. And that felt wrong too."

The sketchbook falls from my fingers and thuds onto the bed. "But...why?"

"I told you," he says, growing redder and redder. "Once I'd met you, you were all I could think about. My Black Widow. And then I wasn't sure I could have you."

"What do you mean?"

Jonny lowers his head. "It sounds stupid but I'd persuaded myself that having Leo's heart meant I couldn't be with you. And then you kissed me and I realized that I couldn't be without you."

It takes a moment for his words to sink in. Then the room stops spinning around me and settles down, although nothing feels the same. I've talked to Teresa about the link between Jonny and Leo so at least I sort of have an answer for this, if nothing else. "I thought about that too and it freaked me out at first." I reach out, wrap my fingers around his and take a deep breath. "But Leo's dead, there's nothing left of him but our memories. It stopped being his heart the moment it started beating for you."

Jonny presses his lips together and nods. His eyes are anguished, darker and more troubled than I've ever seen them before. "I know I blew it. I know I've messed everything up. But it doesn't change how I feel about you so just tell me straight. Do you think you and I could ever

– I mean, should I give up hope now?"

This is it: decision time. I stare down at our fingers, entwined together amid the drips and wires. Can I forgive all the lies, all the pain he caused me or will it always be there, in the back of my mind, a little voice questioning everything he tells me? And I realize that I don't know.

What I do know is that I don't want to go back to the dark days when he wasn't part of my life. It might not be easy at first – it's fair to say we've both got issues – but in time, we could be really good together. It's a risk. But that's the thing about taking risks – you're only half alive without them.

My gaze travels to the sketchbook again; it's like he's captured everything that's good about me and poured it onto the page, all the things I couldn't see for myself. And I remember the day we went to Brighton, when we stood in the middle of the gardens and I wanted him to kiss me so much it hurt.

"No," I say, swallowing hard. "You shouldn't give up hope."

Even after my parents walk in on Niamh and me kissing, I can't quite believe how lucky I am. She should hate me after everything I've done but she doesn't. That, coupled with the news from Mr Bartosinski that I can go home in a few days, means I'm feeling pretty optimistic about the future. All I need now is to sort things out properly with Em and life will be pretty good.

I'm lying back in bed, wondering if she's out of isolation yet, when a familiar head appears around the curtain.

"Femi!" I exclaim, a grin of pure delight crossing my face. It's been months since I've seen him – in fact, I'd assumed he'd moved to another hospital or gone back to Nigeria and that we'd never follow up on our plan to hit

London Super Comic Con. But he's dressed in his nurse's uniform, suggesting he's still working here. "Where've you been, stranger?"

"Where have I been?" he asks, slipping through the door and coming to stand beside my bed. "I've been right here, like always. The question is, what are *you* doing here?"

He reaches for my chart and flicks through the sheets, frowning.

I pull a face. "Slight miscalculation with my medication," I say, hoping he doesn't look too far back through my notes. "I'm better now. But never mind me, how are things with you?"

Femi lowers the clipboard and waves an arm. "They are good. I've been on holiday, can't you tell?"

I grin. Femi's skin is the deepest black I've ever seen. "No."

"Well, I have. Two weeks of rest and relaxation…" His grin fades a bit. "But I am glad to see you, even though I am not glad that you are unwell."

We slip straight back into our old banter. Femi was easily my favourite nurse while I was on the cardio ward and I know Em loves him too. He's impressed at my new-found football knowledge, less impressed when I admit I've let my drawing go a bit. Seeing my sketchbook on the bed, he picks it up and leafs through it, making favourable noises as he goes. "And who is this lovely lady?" he asks, reaching the final page.

Heat rises in my cheeks. "Just someone I met."

His eyes twinkle as he looks at me. "You will be saying next that she is nobody important. Your pencil tells a different tale."

And before I know it, the whole story is spilling out of me like word vomit. I can't stop it, not even when Femi's expression becomes so disappointed that I cringe back into my pillows. When I finish, he is silent for a long time. Then he sighs and shakes his head. "You have certainly made your recovery difficult. And how are things now for this poor girl?"

I picture Niamh waving goodbye, with promises to see each other as soon as I'm well enough. "I think she's okay. Getting better, anyway. We're going to take things slowly."

"Then you are more blessed than you deserve," Femi pronounces. "But then, perhaps we expect too much of you. Serious illness scars the mind as well as the body."

"I know I got lucky," I say fervently. "I have learned my lesson, though. Once I've seen Em I'll be perfectly happy. Do you know how she's doing?"

Femi's face freezes. "Emily?" he says. "What do you mean?"

"Is she still in isolation?" I repeat. "I went along to her old room and she's not there. She told me she was finished with chemo."

He looks over his shoulder towards the ward door, as though seeking help. When he turns back, his eyes are filled with sadness. "We did stop treating Emily, it is true. But not because she was better."

An icy shudder runs through me, as though someone has just walked over my grave. "What are you talking about? She told me she was in isolation but that you were going to let her go home."

"We did let her go," Femi says gently, "but not in the way you think. I'm sorry, Jonny, I thought you knew. Emily died last Saturday."

The words make sense but I don't understand them, not at first. "Died?" I say, disbelieving. "That can't be right, she messaged me last week. She can't be dead."

But even as I say it, I'm thinking of how ill she looked last time I saw her, thin and bright-eyed with fever. Did I swallow the lie about having an infection because I was too self-obsessed to look more closely? And the unanswered messages I'd sent in the last week, the ones my phone said had never been read – I assumed it was because of the new drugs she was on. Saturday? That's when I was re-admitted. Oh God, the staff must have been watching her slip away at the same time they were fighting to save me. I put my head in my hands and try to breathe. I can't believe this is happening.

"Didn't you get the letter she left you?" Femi asks.

"It was supposed to be posted to you or put into your file for your next check-up."

Letter? Still reeling, I raise my head. "I never made it to my next check-up. I ended up here instead."

Femi presses his lips together, then crosses to the door. "Wait one moment. I will be back."

All the time he's gone, I'm replaying the last time I saw Em, wondering if there was some hidden distress call I was supposed to pick up on and missed. If there was, it's as elusive now as it was then. I have no idea why she hid the truth about her condition from me – that was always our deal: total, brutal honesty. And all right, I didn't tell her everything that was going on with Niamh and me but that was pretty minor compared to this. Maybe her letter will make some sense of it all. God knows I can't.

When Femi comes back, he's holding an envelope. He hands it to me, sombre-faced, and tells me he'll give me some space and to call if I want him. Then he heads back to the corridor and I can hear his distinctive voice murmuring to the other nurses. He'll be warning them to keep an eye on me, I think, as I turn the sealed white envelope over and over in my hands, in case I do anything stupid. And I think to myself that being stupid is fast becoming what I do best.

The first thing my fingers find is the friendship bracelet I bought Em from Leo's fundraiser, the one with the silver heart. I stare at it for a moment, my throat swelling up with misery, then pull out the letter. It's written on a crumpled sheet of paper. At first, I think there's been some mistake – this isn't a letter at all, it's the drawing of Chemo-Girl I did for Em, the one she'd said they'd forgotten to put back up after she got moved into isolation. But then I turn it over and see her untidy handwriting on the back.

Hey Jonny,
So it looks like you won and I lost. How funny. Do you remember all the plans we made for the Unbucket list? How we'd live harder than anyone, laugh more than we'd cried, try everything once — whatever it took. We never stopped to wonder what would happen if one of us lived and the other didn't. It was all or nothing — both alive or both dead. Trust me to get it wrong.

I know you'll be wondering why I didn't tell you my cancer had come back. The truth is, I kept telling myself it hadn't. In my head, it was a mix-up with the paperwork and they'd been looking at the wrong biopsy. Because I couldn't have gone through all that for nothing, right? If Chemo-Girl couldn't kick cancer's ass, who could?

I'm sorry for being a cranky bitch the last few times you visited — in case you haven't worked it out. I was jealous; pitifully, horribly, intensely jealous that you'd got better and I hadn't. I wasn't a very good friend to you, Jonny, and I'm sorry about that too. It's not your fault you got lucky, just like it's not my fault I didn't. I wish our last get-together had been one of those times where we laughed so much I got hiccups and you turned blue. I wish I hadn't made you leave.

But you mustn't waste a second on regrets and what ifs — let what happened go and move on. Follow these instructions: Take risks — don't let fear hold you back. Do the list — I know you won't want to but you must. And lastly, most importantly of all, learn how to live.

You spent your whole life waiting for a heart, Jonny. I hope you know you always had mine.

Em

When I wake up, it's late. Someone has tidied away my sketchbook, and Em's friendship bracelet is sitting on my bedside table, the silver heart reminding me again of what an idiot I am. My eyes are gritty and sore but that's nothing compared to the ache inside me. I wish I'd fought harder to make things right with Em when I had the chance. I wish I hadn't been so blind, seeing only Chemo-Girl when my friend was crumbling away underneath. I wish she hadn't written that last line, something else I was too stupid to see. But more than anything, I wish she was here so I could look her in the eye and tell her I'm sorry. I'd give almost everything to do that.

The thing about being in hospital is that it gives you plenty of time to think. And one of the things I've realized in the days since I discovered Em had died is this: I don't want to make any more mistakes. If I'm careful, I can have a good life, make my parents and myself proud, and I owe it to Em and Leo to try. Em, because I have a future she would have done anything for, and Leo because he gave me more than he knew he was giving. It's corny as hell but if today is the first day of the rest of my life, there's something I have to do. I should probably have done it months ago. Reaching for my sketchbook, I rip out a sheet of paper and pick up my pen, chewing on the end as I find the right words.

Hi,
You don't know me but this summer, you saved my life. You gave your son's heart up for organ donation and it found its way to me.

I wish I could show you what a difference it has made, how it has changed everything about me. But instead, I will make you a promise, to always look after it and be grateful for its strength and your sacrifice. And I will never, ever forget the way it was given — from the depths of your own deep sorrow and loss, for someone else's future. I owe you so much.

Thank you from the bottom of my — our — heart.

I'll pass it to Femi tomorrow, ask him to give it to my transplant coordinator who'll know what to do with it. And perhaps someday, if Niamh and I make it past my stupidity, we'll tell her parents who I really am.

Perhaps.

"You're sure about this?"

Jonny looks nervous. I don't know why – it's not like I'm a stranger to graveyards, I know the drill. Although, to be honest, it does feel a bit weird – being here with him. It's definitely not a normal teen, *coupley* thing to do. But I couldn't let him come on his own. Not for his first time since the funeral. "Yeah, I'm sure."

Emily's grave stands out for all the wrong reasons. It's new – one of several in a sad little line, each one a stark reminder that life isn't for ever. This part of the graveyard has a recent feel to it, modern even; some of the graves we pass have those faded plastic flowers poking out of built-in pots; others are filled with long-dead stalks, as though the people who cared enough to bring them have gone themselves now. Emily's grave isn't like those. Hers is alive with flowers and attention, overflowing the way Leo's was during those early months. Eventually, this one will become like his is now – tended with the same love and sadness but in a more manageable way – but for now it's the focus of everyone's loss. There's a chain of friendship bracelets looped over the top.

Jonny is quiet as we stand beside Emily's grave. I used to do this sometimes at Leo's, stand in silence, not really sure why I'd come but needing to be there. Except that Jonny knows why he's here: he's come to say goodbye.

The grass is wet. Dampness seeps gently into my boots, which aren't quite as waterproof as I thought. The late November sun is trying to break through the clouds, plunging us from light to shade. There are plenty of other people around – Sunday afternoon is grave-visiting time, it seems. Some exchange murmured greetings but they don't speak to us, respectful of our silence.

Jonny is stood a little way in front of me, gazing at Emily's name. After a few minutes, he crouches down, reads a few of the plastic-coated cards. Most are water-stained, some illegible. I remember that too. And then he reaches inside his coat, pulls out a transparent A4 pocket and places it carefully among the flowers. It's a drawing of Emily, with a big smile, crazy dark curls and dancing eyes.

It isn't Chemo-Girl, it's something altogether more heartfelt and intimate. It's perfect.

"You know it will get ruined out here," I say gently.

"Then I'll do another," he replies, without looking up. "I can't stop drawing at the moment anyway."

He lapses into silence. The sun gives in to the clouds and a fine drizzle starts to fall, coating us slowly in silvery droplets. "It's okay to miss her," I say.

"I know. It's just—" He breaks off, stares into the distance. "The last time I saw her, we argued. I thought it was about something stupid but then she wrote me a letter and now I don't know what to think."

"What did it say?" I ask, even though I'm not sure I want to know.

"She gave me some instructions – that I shouldn't be afraid to take risks, that I should finish the Unbucket list and really live." There's a momentary hesitation, a second where all I can hear is the almost inaudible hiss of the rain. Jonny sighs and gets up, coming to stand beside me. "And she told me I'd always had her heart."

My stomach twists at the last part. What is he saying, that Emily loved him? Does that mean he would have done things differently if he'd known? "Oh."

He runs a hand through his hair, turning the shimmering droplets into a slick. "Why didn't she tell me before she died? Why wait until I couldn't ask her what she meant?"

I try to put myself in Emily's place, in love with Jonny but knowing she was dying and I think I understand. "Because you had no future together. Because she couldn't promise you anything but pain. Because she had no time."

Jonny nods, then looks me straight in the eye. "Or maybe because she knew I couldn't return the gift. I think she saw I loved you."

His expression is a mixture of sadness and hope, so poignant that I want to hug him tight there and then. Just like that, the tension in my stomach evaporates.

He holds out a hand. "So what do you think – want to help me follow Em's instructions?"

I stare at his drawing of Emily, imagining her writing the message to me I've never told Jonny about, the one asking me to give him a chance. Did she know, even then, how he felt? Did she risk it anyway? And unbidden, an image of Leo pops into my mind, standing on the beach in Devon, his blond hair whipping in the wind, a playful challenge on his golden face. *Go on*, he seems to be saying, *I dare you.*

Blinking hard, I shake away the moisture that's part rainwater, part teardrops, and focus on Jonny, waiting for my answer. "Yes," I say, slowly reaching for his hand. "I think I do."

He presses my fingers to his lips and the warmth seems

to fill every part of my body. "Good," he replies. "Because I don't want to do it without you."

And in my head, Leo smiles.

READ ON, AS AUTHOR, TAMSYN MURRAY, DISCUSSES HER REAL-LIFE RESEARCH

A NOTE FROM THE AUTHOR

Before we begin, I need to go right back to September 2012. Another writer shared a link about a teenager who had tragically died while on holiday and whose organs had been donated. My own son was less than a year old then and something about the story touched me – I couldn't stop thinking about the family of the boy who died, and how they took some comfort from knowing he was saving others, which in turn made me wonder about the people he might help. Before I knew it, the germ of a story had grown: Jonny arrived first, then Leo and finally Niamh (although she wasn't Leo's twin at first, and she was a boy, which would have made the story quite different). It took me until 2014 to complete a first draft – I cried a lot while writing it – and even longer to craft it into something approaching the book I wanted it to be. Finally, in 2016, I'm happy with it.

You can't write a book like this without doing A LOT of research. I began online, researching Jonny's heart condition, which led me to a miracle of modern medicine: the Berlin Heart. I wanted to understand what life in hospital might be like for children who have life-threatening, long-term illnesses, so I watched several of the BBC's Great Ormond Street Hospital documentaries, including one about child heart patients and one about children with cancer.

Once I knew Jonny's story, I began to think about Leo, so I contacted the NHS Blood and Transplant team, who put me in touch with their Associate Director, James Neuberger. He helped me enormously, from things like using the correct language to understanding how the complex and sensitive subject of organ donation might be raised, and even whether Jonny might be able to find out who his donor was: and yes, it is possible and does happen.

I lost count of how many hours I spent on the NHS website, researching things like blood and tissue types and how these might impact Jonny's story. I researched blood clots and strokes too, as these are a particular risk to Berlin Heart patients, and I read a lot of blogs written by teens and adults who'd had a heart transplant, which helped me to understand how life changes with a new heart. One truly inspiring recipient has run the London Marathon fifteen times since his operation!

Emily has acute myeloid leukaemia, which is a particularly aggressive form of cancer. I spent a lot of time researching her complex treatment regime because it happens in three distinct stages and is very hard going on the patient.

Leo's hospital scenes were the toughest to write, partly because they were so emotional, but also because they were quite hard to research. Specific medical conditions and their treatments tend to be well-documented online, but peoples' experience of A & E, and the way medical staff interact with the families of patients in intensive care, tends not to be. So I used what experience I had and imagined myself in the shoes of Leo's family. I also managed to find some NHS Organ Donation staff-training videos, which helped me to ensure the conversations Leo's family has with the medical staff in the hospital were both sympathetic and realistic. And I had expert advice from a number of doctors.

Niamh's story came almost entirely from my own experience of grief and depression. Like most people, I've lost family members, and I tapped into that sense of loss and desolation, plus the way families react. I've also lost someone to suicide, as well as helping a loved one with depression, so I was especially keen to ensure this story strand was both sensitive and real. The Samaritans were really helpful with this too – they read the scenes and advised me where I could improve things. I also wanted to capture that intense love-hate feeling that siblings often have. Niamh is not always likeable because of her conflicted emotions over Leo and her parents, but I think she's more believable as a result. This mostly came from my own experience of family relationships.

Lastly, I thought a lot about what our hearts mean to us. Jonny asks his consultant whether he'll feel any different when he gets his new heart and I realized early on in my research that this was a common question among heart transplant patients; I think it really taps into the belief that our hearts are more than just the pump that keeps us alive. They are the place our soul lives, the part of our body that decides who we love and who we really are. If you get someone else's heart, would you absorb some of their identity – their hopes and dreams and emotions? Might you even start to become them a little?

That's partly what happens to Jonny. Being so ill has meant he doesn't know who he is and I think his obsession with brilliant, golden Leo is entirely understandable. Deep down, he's also afraid that he doesn't deserve his second chance, that he's somehow not worthy of Leo's gift and so he tries to be more like him as a result. As I wrote and researched, it really made me aware that life after transplant is not easy – as well as joy and relief at being well, there's a lot of medical and emotional fallout to deal with, which I hope I have been able to explore through Jonny.

IF YOU HAVE BEEN AFFECTED
BY SOME OF THE ISSUES
RAISED IN THIS BOOK,
THE FOLLOWING ORGANISATION CAN HELP.

Samaritans are available round the clock,
every single day of the year.

Talk to us any time you like in your own way and
off the record, about whatever's getting to you.

Call us free any time on 116 123
Or email jo@samaritans.org
Visit us: find your nearest branch on
samaritans.org

TAMSYN MURRAY writes for all ages from picture books to YA, including Usborne's *Completely Cassidy* and *Tanglewood Animal Park* series. Her YA *Afterlife* series was published to widespread critical acclaim, with *My So-Called Afterlife* Highly Commended in the Teenage Booktrust Prize, and *My So-Called Phantom Lovelife* shortlisted for the Romantic Novelists' Association YA Romantic Novel of the Year.

ACKNOWLEDGEMENTS

This book has been four years in the making and, as you might suspect, the list of people who have helped me along the way is lengthy.

I'll start at the very beginning, with Jojo Moyes, who shared a link that planted the seed that would grow into an impossible-to-ignore story. From there, I went to James Neuberger, Associate Medical Director (Organ Donation and Transplant) of NHS Blood and Transplant, who very patiently answered my stumbling, clumsy questions when I didn't really even know what I was asking, and shared his expertise in a way that helped me so much. Later, he read what I'd written and set me straight again – I cannot thank him enough for his grace and generosity. I also need to thank Dr Jo Cannon, now a bestselling author in her own right, for helping me to frame the early parts of the book when I was still working out how an emergency like Leo's would be treated. I owe a massive debt to Dr Philippa Berman, who read the complete book and corrected my many mistakes – thank you. And lastly, I must thank Lorna Fraser of The Samaritans, who advised me on Niamh's mental health storyline. All these kind medical professionals did their best to make sure I got it right and I am humbly grateful for their help. Any mistakes or blurring of medical lines are totally down to me, not them.

I am incredibly lucky to have a wonderful tribe of writer friends to support and encourage me. Chief among these is Julie Cohen, who read an early draft and gave just enough tough love to make me turn my story into the book it is now – pretty sure I still owe her a drink for this. Hot on Julie's heels are Rowan Coleman, Miranda Dickinson, Kate Harrison and Cally Taylor – my heroes and inspiration every single day. I'm honoured to count the following wonderful writers among my friends and thank them for their unfailing support and advice: Jill Mansell (whose books I read and adored for more than twenty years and who I still can't quite believe is my friend), Rosie Walsh (AKA Lucy Robinson), Alexandra Brown, Milly Johnson,

Katy Regan, Chrissie Manby and Meg Sanders. My #UKYA writer friends have been equally amazing – special mentions to Keris Stainton, Susie Day, Keren David, Sophia Bennett, Cat Clarke, Luisa Plaja, Katie Dale, Rachael Lucas, Lisa Williamson, Liz Kessler, Zoe Marriott, Rhian Ivory, Lisa Glass, Clare Furniss, Ruth Warburton and Rae Earl. Huge apologies to the unsung heroes I haven't mentioned – you know who you are: just keep swimming. Much appreciation to Elaine Penrose for her unfailing bookselling support. And special thanks to Katina Wright of Creatively Well for making more than fifty bespoke friendship bracelets just like the one Jonny gives Em – I hope the finger cramps have gone now.

Enormous thanks to my agent, Jo Williamson of Anthony Harwood Ltd, for guiding every step I make – we've come a long way since 2008! At Usborne, I need to thank my superstar editor, Stephanie King, for caring as much about Jonny and Niamh's story as I did – her TLC and attention to detail made this a book I am so proud to have written. Many thanks to Rebecca Hill, Anne Finnis, Sarah Stewart and Becky Walker for the extra editorial support. Thank you to Hannah Cobley for the gorgeous cover design and Sarah Cronin for the special touches inside. I'm very grateful to all Usborne's PR and Marketing team for putting up with me – especially Amy Dobson and Stevie Hopwood.

And lastly, my undying thanks go to my babies, T and E, for indulging a mother who spent a long time crying over imaginary children. You taught me what love truly is and I could not have written this book without being able to cuddle you when it all got a bit much. My heart is entirely yours, always.